Blackwing Wolf

(Kane's Mountains, Book 2)

T. S. JOYCE

Blackwing Wolf

ISBN-13: 978-1539057529
ISBN-10: 1539057526
Copyright © 2016, T. S. Joyce
First electronic publication: September 2016

T. S. Joyce
www. tsjoyce.com

NOTE FROM THE AUTHOR:

This book is a work of fiction. The names, characters, places, and incidents are products of the writer's imagination or have been used fictitiously and are not to be construed as real. Any resemblance to persons, living or dead, actual events, locale or organizations is entirely coincidental. The author does not have any control over and does not assume any responsibility for third-party websites or their content.

Published in the United States of America

First digital publication: September 2016
First print publication: September 2016

Editing: Corinne DeMaagd
Cover Photography: Greenowl Photog
Cover Model: Shade Moran

DEDICATION

For you.
Yes you, holding this book.
I am your fan.

ACKNOWLEDGMENTS

I couldn't write these books without some amazing people behind me. A huge thanks to Corinne DeMaagd, for helping me to polish my books, and for being an amazing and supportive friend. And to the team who helped me on this cover, Greenowl Photog and Shade Moran. I couldn't have asked for a better Dustin for the cover, and I know the work that goes into one of these shots is immense. To my little team, my family, who put up with so much to share me with these characters, you have my heart.

And last but never least, thank you, awesome reader. You have done more for me and my stories than I can even explain on this teeny page. You found my books, and ran with them, and every share, review, and comment makes release days so incredibly special to me.

1010 is magic and so are you.

ONE

Dustin Porter didn't want to do this. In fact, he would rather do literally anything else in the world than sit in the dark woods waiting on his pack to show up. Axton was going to bleed him.

Dustin leaned up against his Nissan GT-R. He'd bought it in all black, because the ladies loved dark and sleek. That, and it matched his wolf. Dustin checked his watch and smoothed his shoulder-length hair out of his face. This was just like his brother to make him wait on his punishment. It was just like when they were kids, and their mom got called into the principal's office to discuss whatever trouble he and Axton were in. She'd beg Mr. Sheldon not to suspend them *again*, then jam a finger at them and say, "Just wait until your father hears about this. See you at home, boys." Ugh, those days sucked balls. It would've been easier to get the beating over with, but no, he had to endure the rest of the school day and then sit around waiting for Dad to get home to wallop him.

Axton was just like Dad. That wasn't a compliment.

The sound of a truck engine rattled the woods and drowned out the gently flowing river in front of Dustin. Already he felt the urge to expose his neck just to save himself from pain. Dustin inhaled deeply and plastered a smile on his face, then turned to greet the bouncing headlights.

Axton angled toward his GT-R but didn't slow down. Fuck. Dustin put his hands out. "Not the car!" It was the one material possession that meant anything to him.

Axton gunned it, laughing out the window like a psychopath, the dick. Dustin stepped in front of the car and waited for the hit. God, this was going to hurt, but Axton wouldn't kill him. Probably. Axton slammed on the brakes and skidded to a stop just inches away from Dustin. Dust kicked up in swirls around him. The door to the old truck swung open so hard it banked back, and Axton let off a string of curse words that would curl the hair of their granny wolf.

"Hey, what did the door ever do to you?" Dustin joked.

Axton pinned him against the side of the car and slammed Dustin's head backward. His brother was the opposite of him. He used to be tall, dark, and handsome where Dustin barely made six foot and was stockier with sandy-blond hair. All the ladies used to drop their panties for Axton, but not anymore. Harper Keller had burned him so badly that one side of his face looked like melted metal. His hair hadn't grown back either. His eyes glowed silver as though his wolf was already wanting the fight, but that was just Axton now. He'd been a loose cannon before, but now he wasn't right.

"You had one fuckin' job to do," Axton ground out.

"Dude, breath mint."

"Jokes? Seriously?" Axton yelled. He squeezed his fist around Dustin's throat, cutting his air off slowly. "I could pop your head from your body right now, and do you know what I would feel? Nothing."

The threat hurt in ways his soulless brother would never understand.

"All you had to do was get in the crew. That's it. So imagine my reaction when it's announced that the Blackwings registered a bear and a panther to the crew, but no fuckin' wolf."

Dustin's vision collapsed inward from the lack of oxygen, but Dustin didn't dare struggle. This is the way it was with Dad, too. Struggle, and he really would kill him. Wait for him to tire of the abuse, and Axton might let him breathe another day. He hated his brother. But he loved him more than anything. He was his alpha. Maybe he should just provoke Axton this time and end the purgatory.

After Axton released his neck, Dustin doubled over, gasping. Rubbing his throat, he croaked out, "They aren't done recruiting. I still have time. Look, they wanted a couple, obviously. Rowan could be breeding and vulnerable soon, and it'll only be the dark dragon protecting the crew. I think they picked a mated pair to recruit because Kane's looking for protective brawlers who care about breeding, too."

"What about your fool-proof way in?" Jace,

Second of the Valdoro pack, asked in a bored voice from where he leaned on Axton's truck.

"Look, Dark Kane knows who I am."

"How do you know?" Axton asked. "And why the fuck didn't you keep from being made?"

"He knew from the moment I walked into his house, Ax. I could see it in his eyes. Could smell his hatred. It'll take time to earn his trust. He knows I'm Valdoro pack. I don't know how he does, but trust me, that dragon has me figured out."

Axton paced away and yelled "fuck!" into the woods. And then he began talking to himself. Or his wolf? "He's made. What do we do now? We could go in there hard, bring the medicine to suppress the dragon, keep him chained up and make him tell us everything about Harper's weaknesses, then kill him. But what if he escapes? What if his mate defends him? We could kill her, too. We're already going to kill them both, but we need information first. They aren't our target. The Bloodrunners are. Can't get close enough to Harper. We keep trying but she's too wary. She won't let us near her. Want to hurt her first anyway. Kill her and we'll be okay again. Take her mountains. It's my territory. Pack territory. Gotta be careful of her fire. Fire. Fire." Axton squatted down and gripped the back of his head. "We'll rip the fire from her belly and kill everything she loves. Hunt like a pack. Work in from the outside. Kill her pets. Learn her weaknesses. Kill the Blackwing Dragons. Kill her crew. Kill her mate. That baby. That dragon baby. That baby."

Dustin frowned at Jace who was watching Axton's conversation with himself with as much worry on his face as Dustin felt. Axton smelled sicker than the last time Dustin had seen him.

Well, at least Dustin understood the plan better now. Axton had been pretty damn vague when he'd ordered him to apply for the Blackwing Crew. Honestly, Dustin had been on this little suicide mission thinking he was just supposed to kill the dragons, not get information about Harper from them first.

"You said you almost killed them," Axton said, standing and slinking closer, insanity in his bright silver eyes.

"Yeah, when the A-Team came after them. I almost had a chance. Kane and Rowan were pumped full of drugs and their dragons were suppressed."

"Who's the A-Team?" Jace asked.

"Oh, that's what me and the D-Team named the asshole shoo-ins for the crew. Except they weren't really there to join. Somebody sent them after the Blackwing Dragons."

"You ain't no D-Team, you dumbass!" Axton barked out. "Don't lump yourself with them. You're pack. You're Valdoro. You're mine. Don't you grow sympathy for those shifters. They're cannon fodder. They're already dead."

Dustin dipped his gaze to Axton's work boots as the faces of the D-Team flashed across his mind. Logan, Winter, Beast...Emma. She was just a helpless human. He didn't like Axton's threat. "What did they do wrong?"

"Weak!" Axton yelled, spittle flying from his lips. "You're so fuckin' weak. You stink of it. Dad was right. Fucking submissive werewolf, what good are you? No good to me. You fail and fail and fail. Where were you when we tried to kill that Bloodrunner bitch, Lexi? Huh? I didn't see you hunting. I looked around and, poof, my own flesh-and-blood brother has tucked tail and run like a coward."

The heat of fury blasted up Dustin's cheeks. He

hadn't run away. He just hadn't hunted the human because Axton had been wrong to order the pack to murder her. Axton had brought the wrath of the Bloodrunners on himself, but Dustin could never, ever say that out loud if he wanted to stay alive.

Jace stepped closer and ran his hands through his spiked hair. "Look, Dustin, you said they were looking for paired-up shifters. I can get you a female."

"Won't work. They closed down applications."

"Okay," Jace said, "then pair up with a female already up for consideration."

"Emma is the only girl, and she's human."

"Perfect. Manipulate her. Use her. Fuck her, I don't care. Get in the fucking crew so we can move onto the next step of this plan. Look at your brother." Jace gestured to where Axton had wandered off to the edge of the tree line. He was taking a piss and talking to himself. "Losing the pack was hard on him. The loss is too much on his wolf. If he's going to be okay, he has to have vengeance. His wolf needs it to steady out so we can start rebuilding Valdoro."

Dustin didn't like this at all. He'd always gone along with his brother's decisions because he was the dominant sibling. And when Axton took alpha of one of the biggest packs in North America, Dustin had been there to watch him rise, backing him every step of the way. But this? Going against the dragons to get to another equally lethal dragon? And it wasn't Jace or Axton taking the risk. They'd put it all on his shoulders.

"Brother," Axton said, suddenly blurring to a stop in front of him. His eyes were almost lucid and had darkened to the color of storm clouds. When he cupped Dustin's head and rested his own forehead against Dustin's, it almost felt like when they were kids again. When they were friends. His eyes were full of desperation when he pleaded, "Save me, brother." A long snarl rattled Axton's throat, and he closed his eyes tightly. "Save us," he said in a monstrous voice.

And what else could he do? Axton was all Dustin had in this world. He was family. He was pack. "Okay," he murmured.

"Swear on Mom," Axton said, like when they were kids.

Dustin swallowed hard at the pain in his chest. "I swear on Mom."

Axton slapped the back of his head a couple

times—too hard. "Good boy. Now Change. I need to bleed something."

"What?" Dustin asked. He looked from Axton to Jace, but the Second only shrugged.

Axton walked a few paces away and then turned, his eyes blazing white. "Give me your wolf." A cruel smile twisted his face. "First you failed, and then you questioned me. I can't let that slide, and you know it." Power rippled through the air as his brother gave the order. "Change. Now."

Dustin fell to his knees and tried to fight it, but this was part of being submissive, the part he hated the most about himself. It was part of being at the bottom of the pack. He was eternally stuck following the order of monsters. His head snapped back, and a whimper of pain wrenched through his throat as he fought with all his strength. His wolf was being dragged from his skin, though, his bones breaking slowly. Axton was watching with a satisfied smile that said he got pleasure out of watching him hurt. He always had.

Dustin hated and loved him. Hated and loved.

A gray wolf exploded from Axton's body, and Dustin yelled as his own black wolf ripped out of his skin.

And then there was pain.

TWO

Emma stopped sketching the dark, sleek lines of a panther in her journal and narrowed her eyes at the window. A set of headlights had just drifted over, briefly casting a line of bright light through the small opening between the thick black-out curtains.

She slipped off the bed, padded over to the window, and lightly brushed the curtain aside in case it was Beast returning late. He was terrifying at nights, as if his animal was ready to hunt. Nocturnal carnivores even set off her dull human senses.

Dustin parked in front of his room a couple doors to the right. His black sports car skidded to a halt while the rumbling engine cut off in the same second. Idiot probably spent more on that car than she made in three years. It was hot as fuck, though.

When Dustin stumbled out, holding his neck, Emma gasped. In the illumination of the neon motel sign, dark crimson was streaming through his fingers.

"Oh, my gosh," she murmured, but couldn't hear herself, so she bolted for the charger where her hearing aids were nestled inside. With trembling fingers, she placed them in her ears and then grabbed her phone. She dialed Winter on reflex, but on second thought, she hesitated connecting the call. Winter and Logan were Blackwings now while Emma, Dustin, and Beast were still rogue. It shouldn't have mattered, it really shouldn't, but to Emma, it did.

She shoved the cell deep in her back pocket, snatched her key card off the table, and then bolted for Dustin's room. Beast was still gone, shifted into his animal deep in the woods somewhere, so he wouldn't be any help. Besides, that shifter couldn't control himself around other males with injuries. One whiff of the blood streaming out of Dustin's neck, and he would attack. He wouldn't be able to help himself. His animal was broken just like the rest of them.

Emma slammed her fist against the door, but it gave under her force. Frowning, Emma pushed it open to find a bloody shirt had propped the door open. She kicked it out of the way, then clicked the door closed behind her.

Dustin stood across the room at the sink, snarling. "Get out, Emma." His eyes glowed eerily, one ocean blue and one seafoam green. His shoulder-length hair was matted with blood, and there were open gashes all over his bare torso. He had a roll of toilet paper against his neck that wasn't going to do anything but keep Dustin's blood from staining the white porcelain sink.

"I'm going to get some first aid," she said in a much steadier voice than she felt.

"No, don't come back in here. Emma!" he yelled as she bolted for the motel office.

John was working tonight, and he would have something for her. He was a helpful soul, and they talked whenever she needed anything. He'd told her he'd bought a bigger first-aid kit for the motel after Winter had come in injured. Logan had clawed her arm all to hell, and John had been nice about it. He hadn't even kicked the shifters out of his motel, just prepped for more bloodshed. Smart man.

"Hey Emma," John said from behind the

computer desk where he was flipping the pages of a sexy bodice-ripper romance. John was straight as a nail, but he liked reading the dirty scenes. Sometimes she raided his sexy book stash when she was bored.

"Hey John, you know that shifter first-aid kit you ordered?"

His dark, bushy eyebrows arched up high. "You need it?"

"I need it fast," she punched out, doing her best to enunciate her words. The hearing loss made it hard to talk clearly sometimes.

Saying something she couldn't understand, John bolted for the back room. He repeated when he came out again. "Do I need to call an ambulance?"

"No! No, it'll be fine." No more police, or Dark Kane definitely wouldn't let the rest of the D-Team into his crew. She took the large plastic box by the handle and forced a smile. "Thanks, John, I'll bring this back."

"Good luck," he said, worry wrinkling his forehead.

Emma sprinted back across the parking lot. For as much as Dustin had yelled at her not to come back, he was waiting at the door for her. "I can't get it to stop bleeding," he said low enough she barely caught it.

"Talk louder," she demanded, shoving him back into the room. She bullied him into the bathroom, and for as strong and powerful as the werewolf was, he allowed it. Usually Dustin fought everything, so he must've been bad off.

"Let me see," she said, shoving the soaked red roll of toilet paper away from his neck.

Something had damn-near ripped his throat out, and now Dustin was pale as a ghost and averting his gaze away from her, a weak human, as though he was ashamed.

"Who did this to you?" she demanded. "Who?" She shoved him hard on the shoulder. "Did some of the A-Team escape? Did they do this?"

No answer.

Emma yanked a towel off the rack by the shower so hard the fabric snapped at the end. She pushed it against his neck, dug through the first aid kit, and pulled out the packs of sterilized, curved stitching needles and sutures. "Thread this, I'm calling Kane."

"No! You can't call him. Please. Don't call anyone. This is...this is my own thing." Dustin hadn't ever gone this long without joking, and now he was begging her to keep his secrets. Something big was happening. Something bigger than both of them. But he looked so desperate, so serious, and she'd never seen him like this.

Emma blew out a steadying breath. "Dustin, you still have to thread the needle. My hands are shaking too bad."

Dustin frowned and dipped his gaze to where she clenched her trembling fists at her sides. His fingers were streaked with dried blood, but she didn't flinch away when he squeezed her hand. "Okay, I will. Hold the towel."

Emma held it to his neck as he moved them slowly to the counter. He turned, giving her his back—brave for a wolf to do that when he was injured—but Emma was no threat to a man like him. He could snap her neck before she even had the thought to hurt him.

Something rattled just on the edge of her hearing, and she could feel it in the air, some vibration she didn't understand. Carefully, she rested her free hand on the muscular planes of Dustin's back. He was growling, softly. So softly her hearing aids hadn't helped her pick it up.

Dustin ghosted her a glance in the mirror, then turned and presented her with the threaded needle. "Hurry." His hands were shaking now too.

In a rush, Emma went to work on his neck. She hated the blood, but this part she was good at.

"You've done this before," Dustin said, loud enough this time. He was probably trying to keep himself distracted from the sting of the needle.

"This ain't my first rodeo, cowboy."

He flinched under her hand, so she moved closer and tried to be gentler when she pulled the torn skin together.

She talked to distract him. "I used to work nights at a hospital. I was thinking about being a nurse, or maybe a doctor, but changed my mind after a year working the front desk in the ER. I learned a lot though. There was a nice doctor that took me under her wing and showed me the ropes. She was like a mentor, and taught me a lot." Emma shot Dustin a quick look and said carefully, "No claw marks."

"What?"

She blew out a sigh and pressed another stich into his skin. "You don't have any claw marks, so that rules out bears and big cats."

"Stop it. Stop with the guessing. I'm not talking about it."

"Fine, but I want to know what werewolves are doing in the area and why they nearly ripped your throat out, Dustin. This could've killed you."

"Nothing can kill me. I'm invincible," he said through a smirk.

"That's not true. You know it and I know it. The A-Team was annihilated by Logan and Winter. People die, and tonight it could've been you."

"You would've missed me, huh?"

She wanted to claw that grin off his face. It was a fake one. A forced one. It wasn't real, and they'd been through enough during the Blackwing interview process that he didn't have to hide real feelings with pretend bravado. When Emma jammed the needle into his neck, he snarled loud enough for her to hear this time. Fast as she could to distract his wolf from his aggression, Emma pulled the back of Dustin's hair and leveled him with a look. "What's going on, Dustin."

He stood there frozen, glaring down at her with narrowed eyes. "Careful, Human. Some shit is too far over your head, and you shouldn't get involved in things that don't concern you."

"You concern me."

A look of shock drifted over his face, just for an instant, and then his smirk was back. "You wanna fuck now?"

She made a pissed-off *tick* sound behind her teeth and started sewing again. She would have to cut these stitches out tomorrow when his skin was cinched, but he needed these for tonight to stop the damn bleeding.

Suddenly Dustin went down hard. His legs just went out from under him, and he went to the floor. Emma tried to soften his fall, but she was scrawny, and Dustin was densely muscled.

Shit!" she yelled as she went down with him. He was white as a sheet, and his breathing came in shallow pants. A thin sheen of sweat broke out on his forehead, and his pupils were blown.

"Dustin?" she said, slapping his cheek gently.

"Don't leave," he slurred.

"I won't. I won't. I'm here. It's okay. I'll take care of you. Go to sleep, and I'll take care of you."

"My brother." He said it so softly she had to read

his lips, but his words made no sense.

"What?"

Dustin swallowed hard and raised his voice just enough. "My brother did this." He locked his bleary gaze with hers for just a few moments before his eyes rolled back in his head and he went limp on the tile floor.

Emma rushed to finish stitching him, but it was hard to see through her blurred vision. His brother tried to kill him? Emma couldn't imagine Enrique or Lauren ever trying to hurt her, much less rip her apart like this. She'd been lucky with her adoptive family, but clearly, Dustin wasn't as fortunate.

Emma cut off the extra suture, checked his pulse, which was slow but steady, then grabbed a clean washrag from the towel rack. She warmed the tap water, drenched the rag, and hesitated over his limp body. She'd never seen Dustin without a shirt on. He had angel wings tattooed on his chest. They were done well, too, perfectly symmetrical, and showed good skill from the tattoo artist. His sandy-blond hair was flipped to the side, and even in his sleep, his torso was so muscular his abs flexed with every breath. His jeans were spattered in dark spots, but they rode low on his hips, and a strip of red elastic sat right above the waist of his jeans. He had good taste in underwear, so there was that. She'd always been attracted to dark-headed men with dark eyes, but there was something masculine yet beautiful about Dustin. When he was passed out and near death, that was, because he had a mouth on him she wanted to claw off pretty damn often. And she was eighty-four percent sure he was a pervert.

She knelt beside him and cleaned his skin slowly, gently, so she wouldn't re-open any of the newly healing bite marks on his ribs and chest. Dustin was so confident, so quick-witted, she'd assumed him invincible. Plus, she'd seen him fight in his human form before, the first day of interviews when the mob of shifters had surged toward Dark Kane. He'd gone into that fight beside Logan and Beast and hadn't backed down an inch. She hadn't been able to take her eyes off him. She blamed those pretty bi-colored eyes of his. Or maybe the sexy, long hair or his sense of humor.

When his skin was clean of blood and she'd bandaged his neck, Emma dragged him by the feet to the bed. She huffed and puffed, trying to get him up onto the mattress, but it wasn't happening. She worked out to keep up with her people, but Dustin was much bigger than her, and she didn't want to hurt him even more. So instead she yanked the unmade blankets off his bed and created a pallet on the floor for him. A couple of log rolls later, and Dustin looked comfortable enough.

Emma checked his breathing. It was so shallow she couldn't force herself to leave him here alone.

Plus, he'd asked her not to leave.

It was late, and she was exhausted after the adrenaline crash, but she was terrified he would stop breathing in the night. So she stayed awake, watching his chest rise and fall, straining her ears for the sound of breathing. And when her eyes got too heavy to hold open another minute, she draped her legs across his chest so she could feel his breath and slumped her head back against the side of the bed.

In the final moments before she fell asleep, she thought of Dustin's brother. Dustin drove her nuts most of the time, and if she didn't want to slap him ten times in a twenty-four-hour period, it was a slow day, but he was D-Team. And though she would never admit it, Dustin felt like a friend. The most annoying friend she had, but a friend nonetheless.

Something dark and ugly inside of her *hated* his brother, whoever he was.

THREE

Emma cracked her eye open. The ache in her neck was ridiculous, and as she took stock of where she was, it made sense. She was lying on Dustin's pallet and someone had stuffed two pillows under her head. Her neck was basically at a ninety-degree angle, and when she moved, her ear hurt. Her hearing aids were small and sleek, but part of them rested behind her ears and she'd slept on one. She groaned as she sat up, but could barely hear her voice. Crap.

She fiddled with the aids, but both were out of batteries thanks to her not charging them long enough last night and leaving them on.

It was early October now in the Smoky Mountains, and cold, but she felt fine thanks to Dustin who had tucked her in like a child. He'd even shoved the edges of the blanket under her like she was a burrito. On a paper towel next to her on the floor, her toothbrush sat beside her half empty tube of toothpaste and a white paper bag that smelled like it harbored a fruit-filled donut. Maybe she was dreaming. Emma rubbed her eyes and blinked hard, but nope, not dreaming. Everything was still there.

When she sat up, the blanket slipped down past her bare boobs. Emma squawked and yanked the covers back up. Dustin was brushing his teeth at the sink and smiled cheerily at her through the mirror.

"Why am I naked?" she asked, but could barely hear herself and grew self-conscious she was speaking too loud and not enunciating enough. She hated when she didn't have her hearing aids.

Dustin frowned and turned. "You don't remember?" he asked, and clear enough she could read his lips.

Clutching the blanket, she shook her head.

"We fooled around. Twice. I was a stud and you were okay, but we'll improve with time. Your hair looks like a bird's nest."

Emma's mouth plopped open in horror. No. No,

no, no, she wouldn't have slept with Dustin. Not him.

Dustin did look quite recovered now with color in his cheeks. And apparently he'd taken his first aid into his own hands because he'd cut his own damn stitches out. "You said my dick was huge, and I said thank you, and you said I was the best you'd ever had, and I said thank you, and then you asked me to eat you out, and I said, 'it's not my favorite, but you saved my life, so okay—'"

"Dustin! Tell me you are joking!"

Dustin belted out a laugh loud enough for her to hear. "You should see your face right now. You look so dumb. Nice tits by the way." He held his hands up as if he was squeezing them in the air. "Perfectly symmetrical. Do you know how rare that is? You're like a unicorn, Em."

"Again, why am I naked?"

Dustin reared back and looked scandalized. "Because you can't sleep with your clothes on. Who does that? I'll tell you who. No one. You're welcome."

Emma shook her head to rattle out the imaginings of Perv-Wolf undressing her in her sleep. She didn't point out he'd actually slept in his bloody jeans because, at this point, she just wanted to escape. She snatched her neatly folded pile of clothes—undies on top—and dressed as best she could under the covers. "How did you get my stuff out of my room?"

Dustin hunched like the volume of her voice hurt his dog ears. "I told John we were fucking when I returned the first-aid kit, and he gave me the key to your room. What's wrong with your voice?"

Heat blasted into her cheeks, and she ripped her eyes away from his lips because she didn't want to read them anymore. She had never been so embarrassed in her entire life. Dustin had seen her naked!

She stood and bolted for the door, but Dustin was there in a blur, looking confused, hand splayed on the door to keep it closed. "What did I do wrong?" He looked back at the room. "I got your morning shit and food to feed you. I researched what humans eat. Who knew it's the same shit I eat, just less meat, and furthermore, your shirt is on backward." He reached for her. "I can fix it."

Emma slapped his hand so hard it stung her fingertips. And then she signed a long string of curses at him because she sure as hell wasn't going to talk again after he'd made fun of her voice.

His eyes got round as full moons. "What did you just do? Did you hex me? Is that voodoo shit? Take it back! I don't need bad mojo, Emma!" He grabbed her wrists and flopped her hands around, but he was pissing her off, so she yanked out of his grasp, clenched her fist, and blasted it at his jaw like Dad had taught her. Only Dustin ducked neatly, and she hit the door with her knuckles.

"Ooooow!" she howled. He hunched again, covered his ears, then hurried and covered his balls like a genius because she really was considering kneeing him in the groin. Again.

I hate you! she signed. And then she pulled open the door, gave him one last fiery glare, and stomped outside. But she really did need her toothbrush so she turned around angrily. He was there with her toothbrush, toothpaste, key card, and the little baggie of breakfast like a dad sending his kid off to school.

Beast was sitting a few rooms down, leaning against his door and staring at them with so much judgement in his eyes Emma yelled out, "We didn't screw!" And then she snatched the stuff out of Dustin's hand, shoved him as hard as she could, considered snapping her teeth at him, decided against it, and stomped back to her room. Only it wasn't her room because her key card didn't work, and when she looked back at the boys, they were pointing to the room next door. Assholes.

She opened the correct door easily enough and tried to slam it behind her, but it was one of those easy-closing doors that slowed down and clicked gently into place, and everything was stupid.

In a cloud of fury, Emma shoved her hearing aids in their charger and readied for the day. She wanted to maul Dustin. No. She wanted something more severe. She wanted to leave here and never come back and never see him again so she could swallow her embarrassment eventually and move on with her life. It wasn't like Kane was going to let any of them into the crew. Not after he'd only given Winter and Logan invites.

What was she even doing here?

You know what. Stupid subconscious thought it new everything, the smarmy heifer. Truth was, Emma was here to enjoy the sunlight and enjoy the competition of trying to get into the crew. And she didn't hate the D-Team. Well, other than Dustin.

Winter was nice, and Logan wasn't bad. Beast was terrifying but probably wouldn't kill her for fun, and she looked up to Kane and Rowan. She had a good feeling about their crew and felt a strange sense of loyalty to the people she was getting to know here. She could be happy in the territory of the dark dragon until she joined her people again.

She sighed and glared at herself in the mirror, then pulled her honey-colored waves into a high pony tail. Today, she was going to play the stay-far-away-from-Dustin game. She would go into town, fill out job applications, and do her best not to think about the infuriating, sexy, pervy werewolf living a few doors down.

Feeling much better with a plan of action in place, she put in her partially charged hearing aids, clamped her teeth onto the donut, threw open the door, and stepped into the sunlight. At the looming figure near her door, Emma startled so hard, the donut fell out of her mouth and plummeted to the dirty sidewalk.

Dustin caught it before it hit the ground and shoved it back in her wide open mouth. "I don't understand what I did wrong. I got your stuff, bought you breakfast, complimented your tits like the Internet said girls like, and then I went one better and complimented your hair like a gentleman."

"You called it a bird's nest."

"I like birds!"

Beast snorted from where he was still sitting outside his room.

"You can't just undress girls, Dustin. It's illegal."

"Why? Everyone has tits." Dustin dipped his gaze to her cleavage. "I mean, granted, I haven't seen a rack like yours in…well…ever. More compliments!" He lifted his hand like he wanted a high five, but Emma rolled her eyes and walked away.

Dustin followed. "I wanted to ask a question, and I swear it isn't about STDs or what size bra you are. But like, a C-cup at least right? A C? They felt like a C."

Emma took a giant bite of donut and desperately wanted a nap.

"Anyway," Dustin continued, grabbing her hand and pulling her toward his car. "I have an errand to run and I'll let you come with me."

"Why would I want to go anywhere with you?" she snapped, yanking her hand out of his.

"Because it involves a puppy, and the Internet

said bitches love puppies."

"Uhh, *women* not *bitches*, and not every human woman loves puppies."

"But do *you* love puppies?" Beast called. He wasn't helping.

Dustin arched his blond brows and waited.

Emma glared across the parking lot at the vending machines and sighed. She wished she could lie to him, but both Dustin and Beast had those pesky heightened senses and would be able to tell. "Yes, I like puppies."

"Great, our first date."

"It's not a fucking date," she gritted out as Dustin opened the passenger's side of his car like a valet.

"I've seen your tits, Em. It's a date." And before she could yell at him, Dustin shut the door and jogged to the driver's side.

She scarfed down the last bit of her cherry-filled donut as he turned on the engine and rolled down the window. The stereo was blasting AC/DC, but she could still hear Dustin as he pulled away and called to Beast, "Don't eat anyone we like while we're gone."

Beast narrowed his eyes, which were now gold and terrifying, and flipped them off as Dustin peeled out of the parking lot.

"Why do you think people call him Beast?" Emma asked.

"Darlin', he earned that name."

"What do you mean?"

"First, can you not feel him? God, being a human must suck. How do you know who is a danger to you when you meet them? Beast is as unstable as Logan. Both of their animals are thoroughly and irreparably broken."

"And yours isn't?"

"Yeah, but it's different for werewolves. That's all genetics, Sugar Puff." Dustin grimaced. "Ew, I tried Emma, I did. I tried on that pet name but didn't like the taste of it. Babe? Does that work better for you?"

"No pet names, Dustin. And how is it different for werewolves?"

"You tell me, Princess Human, claiming to live in a crew. If you really did live in a crew, you would know werewolves are just naturally badass predators—"

"—murderers—"

"—with superior hunting skills and minds geared for battle. We're born bad. It's accepted.

Predator animals like Logan and Beast, though? Nah. When they break, they *break*. Any moment they can go psycho on you and never level out again. What crew, Perky Nips?"

"Even if I okayed a pet name, Perky Nips would never make the cut. And I'm not from a crew." She stared at his profile to watch his reaction. "I'm from a coven."

Dustin downshifted and slammed on the brakes. They skidded until they came to a stop sideways right in the middle of the road. "A coven? Your people are vampires?" He was yelling.

Emma giggled and relaxed the seat back a few clicks, then put her feet on the dashboard.

"No," he said, shoving her ankles until her tennis shoes hit the floorboard.

"I feel like we're at a place where I can be comfortable in your car, *Babe*." Emma grinned and put her feet back up there.

Dustin narrowed his eyes to dangerous little slits. "Just so you know, I researched that little gesture you did earlier, and you said you hated me. I'm really hurt."

"Dustin, don't pretend anything I do hurts you."

"I am." He eased his foot onto the gas and straightened them out again. "I've done everything in my power to—"

"Annoy the shit out of me and everyone else around you?"

"Well, yeah, but I also shared my Chinese food with you once."

"And I saved your life, so I'm pretty sure we're even. Four Devils Coven, born and raised."

"But you're human."

"And so are my adopted brother and sister. My parents had trouble having babies. My biological parents didn't want me. It was meant to be."

"Why didn't they want you?"

"I was born in Russia. My parents were poor, and they really wanted a healthy child, but I was born with messed up inner ears."

"You were deaf from birth?"

This was getting too personal so she brought it back around. "Beast."

"Oh, yeah, he killed his entire pride."

"What?" she yelped.

"Yeah, he was the king of the lions. A legend. Nobody fucked with him, and he kept a pride for the longest any male in the history of lions was able to. Usually prides switch out alphas every few years just because the males fight all the fucking time, but Beast held a big pride for ten years. Took control of it when he turned eighteen and kept it until a couple years ago."

"Eighteen?" Emma's mind was now completely blown. "Why did he kill his people?"

"Nobody knows. There's a billion rumors, but none of them make any sense to me. Not with what I've seen of him."

"What do you mean?"

"He protects women still. He went after Logan immediately when he'd clawed up Winter's arm. The instinct to protect is still there. And he was fucking *king*, Perky Nips. Why would a king murder his entire kingdom and banish himself to a life of nothing?"

"I don't know," she murmured, baffled. "Why are you driving so slow?" The speed limit was fifty, and he was going twenty-five.

"Because you're human. You're basically a water balloon. One fender bender, and you're donezo."

"Okay, that's not true at all. At least go the speed limit."

"Do you have a death wish? You saved me, now I'm saving you. You're welcome, Shortcake."

"No."

"Shit, I really thought that one would stick." Dustin turned into the parking lot of a local grocery store and announced, "We're here," as he pulled up beside a red minivan.

A pretty brunette was leaned up against the van looking pissed, her eyes tracking Dustin as he got out. Inside the woman's car, a giant dog barked and scratched at the window.

Dustin tried to hug the woman, but she ducked away and ground out, "You didn't tell me he wasn't potty-trained."

"Oh, yeah. Well...he was an outside dog when I stole him from Kane, so..."

"You stole him from the dragon?" the woman screeched.

"Sarah, this is Emma, my new girlfriend. Emma, this is Sarah, my old girlfriend."

Emma explained, "I'm not his girlfriend."

Sarah nodded in understanding. "I gave him a pity blowjob one time."

"That was a pity blowjob?" Dustin asked in an

offended tone. "That was terrible if you were doing it out of pity. I barely came, and you bit my di—"

"Do you want the dog or not?" Sarah asked testily, jamming her finger at the mutt barking behind the window.

"Yeah, give him to me."

"A hundred more bucks for traveling here to meet you."

"I already gave you two grand to take care of him."

Sarah shrugged and crossed her arms over her chest.

"Fine," Dustin muttered, digging through his wallet. He slapped a hundred-dollar bill onto Sarah's outstretched hand.

With a dead-eyed look, Sarah pointed her key fob at the car and hit a button. The side door slowly opened automatically. When it was able, a mangy-looking, long-legged mutt scrambled out. He charged Dustin, his tail whipping back and forth with such excited fury, it blurred. He had an under-bite, patches of fur missing, and he smelled like a wet hamster, but Dustin knelt down and greeted him like he was his best friend. "Gray Dog, Gray *Dog*!" he said in one of

41

those barking voices frat brothers used during drinking games.

"Okay," Emma said, trying to wrap her head around what was happening. "So you said he was a puppy, but this dog is super old and borderline hideous."

Dustin glared at Emma and covered Gray Dog's ears. "Rude."

"And did you seriously steal him from Dark Kane? *The* Dark Kane. The End of Days, the Apocalypse, the biggest and most terrifying shifter on the face of planet Earth, you stole his dog?"

"Well I was supposed to kill him. Stealing felt like a better option at the time," Dustin answered. "Come on, Gray Dog."

"Aw man, he pissed in the back seat!" Sarah yelled, leaning into her minivan.

"Good, now he is nice and empty for the ride back home," Dustin said as he lifted Gray Dog into the back seat of his car. "See you later, Sarah."

"No you won't because the dragon is going to eat youuu," she sang over her shoulder.

Sarah made a good point.

"What the hell are you doing?" Emma whisper-screamed as she sank into the passenger's side. "Dustin, you are going to get yourself killed."

"False, I'm going to get myself inducted into the crew."

"Why is this so important to you?"

"Shut your door. Let's go." Dustin's voice had gone deadly serious in a flash.

Emma refused, but Dustin reached over her lap and yanked on the door handle. She blasted her foot against it and locked her leg. "Tell me, Dustin. Why do you want to be in the Blackwing Crew? Real answer."

"Because it's not a pack!" His eyes flashed blue and green, and then he huffed an angry breath and stared out the front window. "And because I have to."

She got it now. It all made sense, even though Dustin wasn't explaining it well. He was on the run from his pack. His brother must've been a part of that pack and attacked him last night. Dustin was searching for sanctuary in shifters, like she was searching for sanctuary in sunlight.

"Do you really think Gray Dog will get you in?" she asked, shutting the door gently.

Dustin shrugged, his longer hair twitching with the motion. "Don't know, but I'm pretty fuckin' desperate to find out."

This was a side of Dustin she'd never seen before. He wasn't joking or smiling. He looked worried, sitting there with a faraway look in his eyes, biting the edge of his thumbnail, leg shaking in quick succession.

When Emma rested her hand on his tense thigh, he flinched under her touch. Looking down with a shocked expression, Dustin did something that stunned her to stillness. He pressed his hand on top of hers, then grasped it. His eyes sparked with intensity as he lifted her knuckles to his lips. He let a soft peck linger there, then rested both their intertwined hands on his leg again and leaned his head back against the seat rest. "Why do you think they let Winter and Logan in the crew?" he asked quietly.

Emma was having a really hard time formulating an answer because Dustin's casual hand-hold was warm and strong. So steady. It felt good to touch warm skin, not the cold vampire skin she'd grown up embracing. "Because they saved Kane and Rowan from the A-Team. And because Winter's last alpha vouched for her."

"And Logan?"

"I think he made it in because they wouldn't have gotten Winter without him."

"The dragons will be trying to breed soon," Dustin said low.

"Maybe. It will be a huge risk to see if Rowan can carry a pure dragon child, though. Adoption or surrogacy would be safer."

"Either way, they'll need a crew they can trust, not a collection of rogues. They'll want a crew with interest in raising cubs and little dragons. With instincts geared toward protecting the young."

"You think they'll only allow couples in?"

Dustin swallowed hard and looked a little green around the edges, but she didn't understand why. "Forget I said anything," he muttered, settling her hand into her own lap.

Her palm tingled and chilled in the absence of his touch. Behind her, Gray Dog whined and stared at Dustin's profile. For the first time in her life, she wished she was a shifter so she could feel what Gray Dog was feeling. So she could sense whatever reaction Dustin was having. With her human senses, she felt nothing, and now Dustin's face was plastered in that smile he fooled so many with. Not her, though. Not anymore.

"If this doesn't work," she said, "I think you need a plan B." Because she sure as shit didn't want to watch him get burned to ashes and devoured by the dark dragon.

Dustin didn't say anything, only shifted gears and pulled out of the parking lot, aiming the nose of his car toward Kane's Mountains.

Minutes drifted by before he spoke again. "You want to pretend to be mine?"

"What?" That wasn't the direction her mind was going. "I was thinking an escape plan."

"But you think it, too. You think we'll have a better shot at being Blackwings if we work together."

"Work together? Dustin, being in a relationship with someone isn't a job."

"It could be. We could both get what we want— invites into Kane's Crew. And once we're in, we could just…I don't know…stage a big fight and break up or something. No harm, no foul."

"No harm, no foul," she repeated, disgusted. "I'm not going into this trying to trick the dragons. I want to earn my place, not swindle my way into their crew."

Emma crossed her arms, leaned back against the seat, and stared out the window as the October woods blurred by. Pretend to be his? He'd lost his damned mind. She and Dustin were as different as two people could be. Pretending to be in a relationship with him felt like a very, very bad idea. And thankfully, Dustin didn't push her on it. Wise Wolf kept his trap shut and didn't suggest any more ridiculous scam-artist ideas.

Fucking typical werewolf. She was angry. Angry they'd had some sort of breakthrough today, angry she'd begun to feel differently about him, and then he'd pulled this. While he'd slept, she'd cared for his bleeding neck and slept near him, listening to his breathing until her heart knew the cadence. And then she'd been simultaneously irritated that he'd undressed her, but flattered that he'd researched how to take care of her. He'd teased her with first-date jokes, kissed her hand, but then he let it slip that he was exactly the kind of man she'd assumed he was in the first place—a scammy werewolf.

Her disappointment was as deep as a well.

"Your neck still looks like shit," she grumbled

uncharitably.

"Yeah, well, it'll heal up good-as-new eventually."

"You speak as if you've had your throat nearly ripped out before."

Dustin snorted. "You wouldn't survive a single day in a pack. Hell, you probably won't survive in a crew. Do you feed your vamp family?"

"No. I'm their kid, not their feeder, and that was a dick thing to ask."

"I don't understand you."

"As a human or as a woman?"

"Both. You get mad at everything. It's like you're looking for reasons to be pissed. Life is going to be long and dark if you don't switch that shit off."

"Sorry, Dustin, not all of us replace feelings with jokes."

"I don't know what you're talking about."

"You've obviously been through something hard, Dustin. I didn't get you before, but it makes more sense now. You're funny. You make me laugh. You're witty all the time and have a smart remark for everything."

"You're talking like that's a bad thing."

"It is if you're just trying to cover up all your shit,

Dustin."

He snarled loud enough for her hearing aid to pick it up. "So you have me pegged, huh?"

"Yeah, I think I do. You're fireworks, Dustin."

"What the fuck does that mean?"

"You're dark on the inside, but you're popping off pretty sparkly distractions so people don't see who you really are. You cover up all your shadows with jokes. You make people laugh so they don't have a chance to be disappointed with what you are really saying, with what you are really feeling, with what you really are."

Dustin gritted his teeth so hard his muscles jumped in his chiseled jaw. He shifted gears again, hit the gas, and finally he was going the fucking speed limit and beyond. "You have a whole lot of judgement for someone who has issues of their own. You have me pegged? I fucking observe the people around me, too! Princess of the vampires, coveted, sheltered in the center of a coven so no one hurts you or hurts your feelings so you can feel superior. I fucking remember your answer when Kane asked why you wanted to join the crew. Boredom, Emma? Really? Must be nice to have so much free will, but life doesn't work like that for everyone, and it sure as fuck doesn't work like that for me. Never has."

"I'm not judging you, Dustin! I'm telling you, you don't have to be a firework with me. I'm okay with the shadows! I was raised in darkness. The real you scares me less than some plastered, empty smile and hollow eyes. And you're wrong about me."

Dustin shot her an intense glare, then eyes back to the road. To her, then back. "I'm wrong about which parts?"

"All of them. Was I wrong about you?"

Dustin gripped the steering wheel so hard it creaked under his grasp. "Forget what I asked you earlier. I couldn't pretend to care about you if I tried."

"And there it is," she gritted out, shaking her head against the urge to cry.

"There what is?"

"Your ugliest firework. The dark one with all the smoke. The one meant to burn eyes and make people look anywhere but at you. The one where you say something mean and make them flinch away. Success, asshole."

He sped down the gravel hill of Kane's land, going way too fast, but handling his car like it was made to race on loose dirt. He blasted across the bridge, but she didn't want to be in here anymore. Not with him. Not when he'd purposefully hurt her.

"Let me out."

Dustin slammed on the brakes and skidded to a stop near a thin dirt road that led to a clearing for the trailers. He exhaled explosively and said, "Emma—"

"Nope." She shoved open the door and got out, then made her way down the dirt lane, dashing her fingers under her eyes just to make sure none of those stupid tears had betrayed her and leaked onto her cheeks.

Before she even registered that he'd left his car, Dustin was there, a solid wall of muscle, his arms around her, a snarl rattling against her cheek, his chest heaving under her. He was hugging her too tightly, so she was stuck with her arms pinned between them.

"You were right about everything, Emma. All of it. I shouldn't have said that. You're really nice and pretty, and it wouldn't be hard pretending to like you as more than a friend. I just... I just say dumb shit sometimes."

"All the time," she corrected him.

He huffed a laugh and loosened his grip on her. "Yeah, all the time. I think maybe you should stay away from me, Emma."

"More fireworks?"

"No. This one is a warning because you're a friend. Maybe you're the realest friend I've had, I don't know. No one's called me out before. No one's seen through me. The best thing you can do for yourself is steer clear."

Emma frowned and eased back to gauge the seriousness in his eyes. That answer? Dead serious.

He was so close, so warm. He smelled of cologne and laundry detergent. This was the first time she'd been all pressed against a big, strong man like this. Slowly, she slid her arms around his waist. He cocked his head in such a confused-dog fashion, she laughed.

"I don't think friends hug like this," he said, looking thoroughly troubled.

"Okay, let's stop then."

"No!" Dustin cleared his throat and said it again at a lower volume. "No, I think this is fine for just a minute longer. One minute, and then we let go because that would be crossing some friend line that would be totally gross."

"Oh, completely gross. And besides, you're not my type, Wolf. I like dark-headed immortals with cold skin and fangs. Not tall, strapping muscle men with tattoos of angel wings on their chest. What are those for anyway?"

"Does everything need a meaning? I got those to attract—"

"Don't you say bitches."

"—chicks." He grinned cheekily. "Clearly it worked because I can basically feel your lady boner against me right now."

"One of us has a boner, and it's not me." Emma cocked her eyebrow.

Dustin bit back a smile and leaned forward, hugged her harder against his chest as he lowered his lips to her ear. "We could be friends with benefits. Doggy style in the woods. You ever been with a shifter?"

"I don't even like doggy style."

"You would with me. My dick could change your life."

"And there it is." Emma shoved him hard in the chest as he cracked up.

Barking like a maniac, Gray Dog went blasting

53

past them.

"Shit!" Dustin said, the humor fading from his face. "Gray Dog! Come back!"

They both bolted down the dirt road after the dog, but gads, he was fast. She fell behind quickly because, apparently, Dustin had rockets for shoes. And by the time she reached the clearing, and him, she was winded and her legs burned like she'd just finished a marathon instead of a thirty-yard sprint.

"Why'd you stop?" she wheezed out, hands over her head so she could catch her breath easier.

"Because of that," he said in a strange tone, pointing to a doublewide trailer sitting on a concrete slab. No, not at the trailer, but at a furious-looking Dark Kane who stood in front of it, petting Gray Dog, and glaring at Dustin with pure murder in his green dragon eyes.

FOUR

"Dustin, he's coming this way," Emma murmured. She scanned the clearing, but Rowan wasn't here to stop Dark Kane, and neither were Winter or Logan. Shit.

Dustin pushed Emma behind him as Kane strode toward them with unnatural grace. The air filled with a noise she'd only heard in a dinosaur movie. Dustin backed them slowly toward the road, blocking her view completely with his wide shoulders.

"I can explain."

"Dustin Porter, bottom of the Valdoro pack. Attempted murderer of Lexi of the Bloodrunners and assumed murderer of my dog. I've hunted you for months, and then low and behold, your dumb ass shows up on my doorstep asking to get in my crew."

What the fuck was going on? Emma clutched onto Dustin's shirt as he moved her backward.

"Do you know how fucking hard it was for me not to burn you to nothing when I first saw you? Do you?" Dark Kane bellowed.

A crack formed in the ground, splitting the earth between her feet.

"I didn't hunt Lexi. I ducked out before the hunt began against my brother's orders. I couldn't do it. My punishment for abandoning an order was to kill your dog. Axton thought you would catch me, kill me, or I don't know, but I couldn't kill Gray Dog, so I stole him instead. I didn't have a choice! It was get rid of him, or my alpha would take a pound of my flesh. Stop!" Dustin yelled, holding out one hand. With his other, he gripped Emma's hip so hard it hurt. "I brought him back because I want to be part of this crew."

"Change," Kane said in a low, dangerous voice.

"Wait, wait, wait," Emma murmured, sidling around Dustin.

He tried to stop her, but she shook him off and put both hands out to keep distance between the two men. God, she wished Rowan was here. And Winter, Logan, and Beast because she wasn't equipped for this. Dustin was saying something behind her that she couldn't make out since her hearing aids only projected the rumbling sound that emanated from Kane. His black hair was flipped over to the right, exposing long scars on the side of his head, and his green dragon eyes were completely empty.

"Please, Kane, just listen. Dustin's trying to get away from his pack. Look at his neck! Look at it! His own brother tried to kill him last night."

"Change," Kane demanded again, and even Emma—frail human Emma—could feel the power pulse within that order.

When an awful cracking sound echoed through the clearing, Dustin grunted in pain. The air was sparking with something she didn't understand. The hairs raised on the back of her neck as she turned slowly. A pitch black wolf stood there, legs splayed, white razor-sharp teeth bared, eyes blazing blue and green. He was so monstrously big he was almost eye-level with Emma.

"Oh, my God."

Something horrifying was happening to Kane.

His skin was cracking like the ground he'd split open, and underneath there were matted, black scales. Black smoke seeped through the splits before they closed again and then opened wider.

"Rowan!" Emma screamed desperately as loud as she could, her voice echoing across the mountains. "Kane, Kane, listen to me."

The dark dragon didn't even see her anymore as she waved her arms in front of his face. He was smiling, and his teeth were elongating. When two ominous clicks sounded, the air smelled of smoke. Dustin was going to burn if she didn't do something.

"He's mine! Kane!" She turned and ran to the wolf, and threw her arms around his massive neck. "He's mine, and if you take him from me, I'll never forgive you. I'll never be okay. I'll hate you forever, and I will call on the Four Devils Coven to avenge him. I will bring every news station within five-hundred miles into your mountains, and you will never escape this decision you're making. Choose differently!" She dragged in a long, shaking breath. "Please," she begged.

Kane's glowing green eyes flicked to her and then back to Dustin.

"Kane?" Rowan called from down the road. She was running.

Hurry Rowan!

Under Emma's embrace, Dustin's thick neck rattled with a constant threatening growl. His fur was coarse and prickled her face, and she was scared to stand this close to his teeth, but what choice did she have?

All that stood between Dustin and oblivion...was her.

Kane backed up a step, eyes narrowed. "He's yours?" The dark dragon didn't sound convinced.

"Yes, yes, all mine."

"Lie. I can hear it. Why are you lying for him?"

"What's happening?" Rowan asked, huffing breath.

"Change back!" Kane yelled, his voice cracking through the air like the tail of a whip.

Dustin's response was immediate. Emma was shoved backward with the powerful force of Dustin's Change to his human skin. He fell to his knees, and propped himself on one locked arm as he grunted in pain. Every muscle in his body was rigid as if he'd been electrocuted.

"I don't understand," Rowan murmured, her blue eyes wide. "Why is he obeying you like that?"

Kane shook his head and paced away, spat onto the ground, and yelled, "Fuck! You want to know why? Because his goddamned animal already thinks I'm his alpha. I'm not, Dustin, you fucking shit. I'm not your alpha."

"It's not like I told him to obey," Dustin yelled. "You think that was enjoyable for me? Fuck, Kane, you forced a Change twice in one minute." Dustin jammed a finger at Kane who stalked toward Emma. "Get away from her."

"You don't get to tell me what to do!"

"Well, you're worked up, she's human, and you are too fucking close, Kane. Back. Up."

Rowan held her hands out like she was settling a startled stallion. "Kane, he's right."

"Whose side are you on, Roe?"

"The side that doesn't get you thrown into shifter prison. Is that Gray Dog? I thought he was dead."

"He was supposed to be," Emma rushed out. "Dustin was ordered to kill him, but he stole him instead. To save the dog! He's not bad."

Rowan gave them both a deep frown, shifting her

gaze from Emma to Dustin and back again. "You said Dustin's yours?"

Emma nodded so she wouldn't get caught in a lie again.

"Bullshit," Kane muttered. "There's no way these two are a match."

"That's horribly judgmental," Dustin said, standing stiffly. "What? I can't get a hot babe like Emma?"

Kane flung a hand in the air. "No! Because you say shit like 'hot babe,' you make four-hundred dick jokes a day, you're a psychotic *werewolf*, and Emma's too good for you by a lot."

Dustin's mouth flopped open. "Well...agreed, but maybe she feels like slumming it, okay?"

"Okay," Kane said, crossing his arms over his chest. "Then kiss."

"What?" Dustin said, slowly covering his very bare and swinging dick. "I'm naked. No."

"You wouldn't kiss your mate naked?" Rowan asked, sounding more and more confused.

"Whoa there, Cupid," Dustin said to Rowan. "Emma didn't say we were a mated pair. Just that...you know...we belong to each other."

"Also a lie," Kane said blandly.

"We're in the beginning stages," Emma blurted out.

"But he's yours," Kane said, his eyes tightening. "You just threw yourself in front of him to save his sorry hide from me, so convince me. Convince me he's won your devotion because, if so, I'll believe you that he's not all bad. Save his life, Emma. Kiss him."

Balls. She was really going to have to do this. Dustin was extremely naked and looked just as uncomfortable as she felt. This was where their lie was going to become really freaking obvious because she was a terrible actress.

Dustin looked panicked as he glanced at his shredded clothes littering the ground around him, but none of them were big enough to cover his dick. Emma would've laughed if this wasn't so very unfunny.

Slowly, she squared up to him. With both hands covering his nethers, Dustin rolled his eyes heavenward and leaned forward with a pucker. He laid a chaste kiss on her lips and held for a three-count before easing back.

"That was pathetic," Rowan said. "I saw two

parrots kiss better than that before. They were in a pet store that smelled like dog poop. Look around you, supposed love-birds. You're in the Smoky Mountains, in the prettiest country, under the bluest sky."

"With two pervy dragons judging our kissing," Dustin said crossly as he took a step back from Emma like she had cooties.

He was kind of cute when he was all frowny like this. Emma giggled.

"It's not funny." But on the last word, Dustin cracked a tiny grin. "Look, I have first-kiss jitters, and it's not helping you looking at me with your little face all scrunched up like that. You look like a raccoon."

Emma wanted to swat him. "You aren't being romantic right now at all. And you were the one who pulled away. Your kiss sucked, but not literally, because that would imply your lips moved. I would rate that like a two and a half. Three, max."

"Mouthy," he accused.

She arched her eyebrow pointedly and waited. Dustin grinned at the woods and shook his head like he couldn't believe he was doing this. But he slid his hand against her waist and locked gazes on her. She liked this much better. His eyes were dancing, and his smile was that genuine one he didn't give very often.

He twitched his chin up. "Come here," he murmured in a deep, growly voice.

Chills rippled up her spine at his command. She didn't like being told what to do in general, but oh, that was a little sexy. Gently, he pulled her to him. And when she was pressed against his body, he lifted his free hand to her neck and ran his thumb against her cheek. "Three max?" he asked.

"Better beat that if you want to live, wolf," she dared him through a grin.

He released her suddenly. "Nah, I'd rather die than kiss you. You're gross."

Emma went to shove him, but he yanked her arms around his waist, and his lips crashed onto hers. He had a hand on the back of her neck, preventing escape in a way that was so fucking sexy she was pretty sure her system was going into shock. And his other hand...well...it was on her left butt cheek. So Dustin. When he squeezed and lifted, she squeaked. He chuckled against her lips. Oh, this was a game then?

She pushed her tongue past his lips and brushed

into his mouth. When she bit his bottom lip, Dustin jerked, then froze against her. *Aahahahaha, that's what you get.*

Only Dustin had tricks, too. He abandoned his butt-fondle and moved his hand up her back, pressing her against the stone wall of his torso as he pushed his tongue into her mouth, and *oh dear goodness what was happening*? Her body, the little ho, plastered to him like a strip of wet wallpaper. She slid her arms around the back of his neck like this was real. He angled his head the other direction, and there was that tongue again. Holy hell, Dustin could kiss!

Emma got lost. Time meant nothing, only touch. It had been so long since she'd been able to let go like this. It was just them here in the woods, just them in the whole world as Dustin worked her to a slow inferno. His hands were everywhere, so gentle, exploring her body. His boner pressed hard against her belly but he didn't push for more. He kept them slow and steady, building her up until her panties were wet. A soft growl hovered just under her hearing, rattling against her boobs like one of those vibrating beds in cheap motels. She smiled against his mouth and sucked on his bottom lip, bit down softly again, and she was pretty sure he moaned. His fingers slid through her hair and he cupped her head as he walked her backward.

She was supposed to be doing something. A chore sat there on the edge of her mind but geez Louise it was hard to care about responsibilities when she was pressed up against a tree by a molten hot sex pot. Dustin a sex pot? Hell yep, this kiss sealed it. He'd been hiding his sex appeal with all his walls and pervy jokes.

Whoa, his lips felt divine against her neck. He sucked hard. Too hard maybe.

"You're gonna give me a hickey."

"That's the damn point," he rumbled.

Emma giggled and draped her arms languidly over his muscular shoulders. "You're sexy when you aren't talking."

"Thank you. You're sexy when you don't look like a raccoon."

"Fuck you."

"Okay." He ground his erection against her pelvis, and she laughed again. Why was she so giddy? She felt like she'd taken three shots of tequila.

He used his teeth just enough on her neck. Then,

neck satisfactorily mauled, he kissed up her jaw and gave her lips attention again. She'd never had so much fun making out with someone in her entire life.

Emma sighed happily and ran her hands through his hair, pushing it back from his face. One of her hearing aids cut out, but screw it. She still had the other. The sun was high over Dustin's shoulder, casting him in a halo of blinding light. His eyes were glowing brightly.

"Pretty eyes," she murmured.

He brushed his finger under her eye and murmured, "Prettier eyes."

She practically purred. Dustin sure could compliment when he wanted to.

This time, when he leaned down to kiss her, his lips went gentle against hers, plucking at them with such tenderness Emma got lost with him all over again. He hadn't shaved this morning and, at some point, his whiskers had turned from tickling to burning. Emma eased back with a smack, then pecked him again, again, and again until he rested his forehead against hers and ran a light touch over her swollen lips.

I'm hurting you, he mouthed. She couldn't hear

him, which meant her other hearing aid had died. Dangit. She wanted to hear his voice when it was all tender like his eyes were right now.

At the risk of getting embarrassed by her voice when she couldn't hear like this, she pointed to her hearing aids and sadly shook her head.

He looked confused for a moment, but then drew her hand up to his lips. He kissed her wrist, then mouthed clearly, *That's okay.*

Suddenly, he straightened up and looked around the clearing. Easing off her, he froze, a frown darkening his features as he seemed to listen for something.

What? she signed.

Dustin glanced at her, then away again. He grabbed her hand and pulled her from the tree. The sun was farther up in the sky than it should've been.

Oh crap, the dragons! She was supposed to kiss Dustin to prove they were together. To save his life! But right now, she and Dustin were the only ones here. How long had they been locked up like that?

She pressed her fingertips against her throbbing lips as he dragged her at a clipped pace toward where Kane had forced Dustin to Change. He skidded to a stop so hard she ran into the back of him.

Confused, she rested her palm on the strong planes of his back and stepped around him. On the ground, there were two blue folders.

She and Dustin cast each other matching baffled shrugs, and then they both picked one up. Inside, there was official registration paperwork for the Blackwing Crew. In a clear sleeve was a black bear paw beer bottle opener, and in the other pocket was a packet about a doublewide trailer, cost and specs, that looked identical to the trailer already in the park.

"It worked," she said excitedly, hoping it wasn't too loud.

Dustin was frowning at a handwritten note in his, though.

"What is it?" she asked.

His folder looked identical to hers, but he got a scribbled note? And there was no way that was Rowan's handwriting. It was too harsh and borderline ugly. Rowan probably dotted her *I*s with bubble hearts, but this was barely legible.

Dustin shook his head and tossed the folder to the ground. He handed her the note and then ran his hands through his hair. And then he turned and walked down the dirt road toward where he'd parked the car.

Troubled to her marrow, she watched him leave and then read the note silently.

Dustin,

You are invited to join my crew on a few conditions. One, you come clean about why you are really here, and do it quickly before I lose my patience. Two, you will only be able to turn in your registration paperwork to the courthouse and officially become a Blackwing if you secure a claiming mark from Emma. Or you can get married, whatever she wants. You will tether yourself to someone decent before I will let you around my crew or my mate. Three, the singlewide isn't an option for you. You can get a doublewide and share it with the woman YOU BELONG TO. Have a fucking fantastic day. You were not my choice. Thank Rowan for picking you, and thank Emma while you're at it for saving you from me. I still want to eat your ashes.

The End of Days.

Kane was pissed if he signed his own hate-letter

as *The End of Days*. The media referred to him like that often, but Emma had seen him get furious when Dustin called him that once.

This sucked. Their little couple plot had worked, but way too well. Marriage? Claiming marks? Living together? That was not at all what they'd bargained for.

This wasn't a crew invite after all.

Smart and savvy dragon that he was, Dark Kane was calling their bluff.

FIVE

When a knock sounded on the door, Emma struggled into her green silk spaghetti-strap shirt as fast as she could. She threw open the door. A tiny twang of disappointment settled in her gut that it was Winter and not Dustin.

"Geez, don't look so happy to see me," said the black-haired woman with the laughing, smoky eyes.

"Sorry," Emma said, adjusting her left hearing aid.

"You ready?"

"I think so. Is this okay to wear tonight? With that jacket?" She pointed to the coat draped on the bed.

"Hell yeah, you look hot." Winter was good about

enunciating in case Emma couldn't catch all her words. She always had been. The panther shifter was sensitive in ways the boys sometimes weren't.

"Are you mad at me?" Winter asked.

"What? Of course not."

"Yeah, but it's been radio silence since Logan and I got our invites into the crew. Even when I text you, you don't respond most of the time."

Now she felt like a real crap friend. Emma hugged Winter's shoulders and rested her chin on one. "I didn't know how to feel. You and Logan felt separate from the rest of the D-Team."

"But now it doesn't have to be like that. You're going to be part of the crew too."

So that's why Winter had asked her to go out for drinks. Rowan must've spilled the beans. "It's not so simple. There are…conditions."

"Like what?"

Emma laid back on the bed and heaved a sigh. The ceiling fan swung around in lazy circles above her, slow enough she could track the movement and not get dizzy. "Dustin and I can only be crew if we are a couple."

Winter laughed really loud and settled on the

bed beside her. "You and Dustin?"

"It's a long story. Everything just got so messed up, and Dustin is my friend, maybe more, I don't know, but not that much. Not enough to commit to for a place in the crew. I tried to talk to him about it, but he's freaking out, won't even talk to me, and I don't know what to do."

"I'm sorry, I'm still kind of reeling over the fact you are having boy problems with Dustin."

Emma rocked up and muttered, "I need a drink." She shrugged into her jacket and checked her skinny jeans and heels one last time. She'd worn her hair down and curled tonight and had done her make-up. Why? Hell if she knew. Dustin had dropped her off at her room and disappeared for the entire day. She'd texted him once to no reply. It stung, and she made a mental note to reply whenever Winter texted, no matter what.

"Emma, are you okay?" Winter asked. Her delicate eyebrows were drawn down with concern, and a sudden urge washed over Emma to smooth them out. Winter shouldn't be worrying. She was newly mated, newly claimed by Logan, newly inducted into the Blackwing Crew. She should be riding a high, not upset over the stupid situation Emma and Dustin had created for themselves.

"I'm fine. I'll be even better after a shot of tequila."

"Thata girl," Winter said, grinning. She led the way outside, but when Emma laid eyes on Dustin, she skidded to a stop so fast she nearly rolled an ankle.

His hair hung in his face as he stared down at the ground, but at her sharp inhalation of breath, he jerked his gaze to hers. He was standing against his car, hands in the pockets of his dark jeans, a navy V-neck sweater clinging tightly to the curves of his muscular chest and arms. And there was that fake smile back on his lips. "Daaaaamn ladies, lookin' downright fuckable tonight."

"You're the worst at compliments," Logan said from the open window of his truck. "Say that to Winter again, I dare you."

Beast climbed into the back seat of Logan's truck and muttered, "I hate all of you. Let's go."

Dustin's empty smile stretched wider. "You heard the Beast. Let's do this." He gave Logan the finger and climbed behind the wheel of his car.

Emma hesitated. Was Dustin still freaking out?

Was she supposed to ride in the back of Logan's truck with Beast, or in Dustin's car?

Dustin dragged wolf bright eyes to her and nodded his head toward his passenger seat. Okay then. She offered Winter a little wave and made her way to Dustin's car. When she was buckled, he pulled out of the parking lot behind Logan's truck, but took a right where Logan had taken a left.

"I thought we were going to the bar."

"Let them go to the bar first and have a few drinks before we get there. Then they won't care about swindling every detail from us about what happened today."

Okay, that was actually really clever. "You aren't as dumb as you look."

"Thank you. What are you hungry for?" he asked conversationally.

"I'll eat when we go to Drat's."

"Your stomach growled, and for some stupid reason all I can think about right now is feeding you like a freaking mommy bird with a helpless freaking baby."

Emma scrunched up her nose. "No thanks to all of that."

"You shouldn't drink on an empty stomach."

"Okay, *Mom*."

"This is a gross conversation. We made out today. A lot. Just pick a place to eat so we can talk and get all of this out of the way."

She sighed and watched the neon lights of the main drag drift by. "I don't know, Dustin. I'm so over fast rood right now. I think I've gained six pounds since we moved out here because motel living means hamburgers at least once a day. I don't feel like fast food."

"You don't like fast food?"

"Not right now. I've been eating it for weeks. It's too much grease."

"Well, grease gives it flavor."

"I don't have your werewolf metabolism or iron stomach. My pants are fitting too tight."

"A, I like your pants fitting too tight, and two, you have clearly gained all the weight in your tits. Win, win. Are you really trying to watch your figure?"

"Kind of. I don't want to buy a whole new wardrobe."

Dustin growled and pulled into a gas station parking lot. The inside was clearly closed, but he parked in the darkest corner of the lot where the streetlight was burned out. "Tonight is my last night here."

"What?"

"I packed all my shit already, but this is for the best. Trust me."

"Trust you?"

"Yeah."

"I trusted you earlier today with your stupid plan to bring Kane Gray Dog, and I trusted you when you said they were only recruiting couples. And then you left me to reel on my own instead of talking to me about what happened. And so you know, I was planning on leaving, too. Not tomorrow, but soon. The heat is too much for me, too. I'm not a relationship kind of girl."

"Lie. You just lied. I could hear it."

"Where will you go? Back to the Valdoro Pack?"

Dustin huffed a laugh and stared out his window. "I can't join the crew, and I can't go back to my pack."

"So...where?"

"I don't know yet. I'll figure it out when I get there."

"Why so soon? Kane's terms didn't give a

timeline."

"Because I can't be your boyfriend or mate or husband or whatever we're supposed to be."

"I know that. You would be the worst boyfriend."

Dustin arced his gaze to her and scoffed, but she was ready with a smile. The corners of his lips lifted and he played along. "Literally, the worst boyfriend."

"I think I heard you snore last night."

"Yeah, probably, since I was dying and all, you judgy judgerton. And you had really cold feet when I spooned you."

"Wait. You spooned me?"

"Fuck yeah, you were naked."

"Dammit, Dustin, I was naked because you took my clothes off!"

"See? This angers you for reasons I still don't understand. The literal worst boyfriend."

Emma snorted and laughed. "I mean, you're a werewolf. Do you even pair up?"

"Hell no, not if we can help it."

"And I'm destined to be a vamp someday. I'm in it for the eternal life."

"I can give you an excellent experience with my penis, but I cannot grant you eternal life."

"You drink whisky, I drink tequila..."

"Oh, we have nothing in common."

Emma shrugged and pitched her voice higher. "So we made out a little..."

Dustin sucked air between his teeth in a hiss. "A lottle, but friends do that sometimes. Right?"

"Well, not like we did, but we can go back. We'll just make fun of each other like we used to, and I'll call you names a lot, and you can just keep doing all the annoying shit you do and stop complimenting me."

"Done. Giving compliments makes my balls shrivel up. Like tonight, your hair?" He shook his head but was cracking an even bigger smile. "Okay, it looks sexy as hell, and I want to play with it, but by play with it, I mean pull it while I'm fucking you senseless, but I swear that's the last compliment I'll ever give you again."

She rolled her eyes to the roof of his car and laughed. "That was a compliment? Okay, last one... You're a really, really good kisser. I mean...out in the woods today?" She arched her eyebrows at him. "A-game."

"I know, right? Credit where credit is due,

though—I had a really good partner. You have those little blowjob lips that are just so suckable."

Emma clamped her legs tightly closed because talk like this was getting her revved up again. "Your dick is really big. I know I called it a Vienna sausage before, but you were right. It's way more than a bratwurst."

"I thought we weren't complimenting anymore. Okay, your vagina is probably really big."

"Nope, that's horrible. That's not a compliment at all."

"No?"

"Nope. The worst."

"Okay, officially friend-zoned again. Those fantastic kisses were just some beginner's luck, so we can do this for a few more days—just hang out, do the friends thing, back off from everyone expecting some big romantic story from us. Maybe if we break up gently, Kane will forget those stupid conditions and let us in anyway."

"Perfect. That's the perfect plan."

Dustin tapped his palm on the steering wheel and nodded once. "I feel much better now."

"Great, can we go to the bar now?"

"First, I'm going to buy you hamburgers to make your tits grow, like a good friend."

Emma giggled as he pulled out of the parking lot. She'd missed this easy rapport with Dustin today. The first day she'd come to interview for the crew, she'd liked him the least of them all. He was a mouthy playboy she hadn't understood, but over the weeks, he'd turned it around and surprised her with his layers. And since she'd tended to his neck injury, he'd turned into this delicious mystery she wanted to unravel slowly.

Dustin pulled them through the drive-through of a fast food burger joint, ordered way too much, then drove ten minutes down winding mountain roads to an empty parking lot.

"We could've eaten in the parking lot of the restaurant," Emma muttered, digging through one of the bags as her stomach growled again.

Dustin swatted her hand and yanked the bag away. "Patience, and besides, you're a mess when you eat. It's like watching a vulture feed. You aren't eating in my car."

She shoved his arm and swung the door open. "That was rude."

"That was honest." He made gulping sounds and a ridiculous eating face.

Emma giggled and shook her head. "Not funny. I'm cute when I eat. No one has ever complained before."

"Because you lived with blood suckers. They don't know what dinner manners are. They probably think you're normal. Grab that, will ya?" He jerked his head at the trunk of the car that he'd popped open.

There was a thick blanket and a pillow in the back.

"Do you sleep in your trunk often?" she asked innocently as she pulled out the blanket.

"Har har, no. I sleep in the back seat when my pack mates are being assholes." His voice had gone all serious, though.

"You know what I've noticed?" she asked as they walked along a winding pathway right beside the river.

"That I'm ruggedly handsome and hilarious and would provide fantastic genetic material for your future children? I mean, I'd make a horrible baby-daddy, but our pups would be cute as fuck."

"Uh, no, since we literally just had the friend-zone talk. No, you talk louder for me now. Clearer. I still have to read your lips a lot, but when I first met you, I was confused half the time because you murmured and wouldn't enunciate."

"Huh." Dustin cast her a sideways glance, and his eyes reflected unnaturally in the moonlight. "Really? I feel like I'm talking the same as I always do."

"Nope, I noticed the difference. Trust me, it's a big change." She bumped his arm. "It's a good change for me. You have a nice voice."

"Compliment! We should make a compliment jar like a swear jar. Like…every time we say something sickeningly nice to each other, you have to give me a blow job."

Emma blasted a surprised laugh and hugged the blanket closer to her chest. "You're ridiculous."

Dustin got quiet, and as he set up their blanket on a flat field of grass overlooking the water, he got a faraway look and a slight frown to his features. When they were settled and dishing out food, he said something that surprised her down to her bones. It was a soft admission, as if he didn't know if he wanted her to hear or not. "You have a nice voice, too."

"What?" she asked, watching his lips carefully. Those lips...so sensual, and she knew what they could do against hers, but now they rained down words that got the butterflies going crazy in her stomach.

"I said you have a nice voice, too. I like it."

Heat burned her cheeks, and she ducked her gaze as she admitted, "I hate it. I worked really hard in speech therapy to get where I am, but someday I want a normal voice. One I can hear perfectly so I can sound like other people. I want to sing." The heat spread to her ears on that last admission, so she cupped her hands over them to hide the blush.

Slowly, Dustin leaned forward and pulled her hands away. "Did you just give me something big?"

She nodded, still unable to meet his gaze.

Dustin scooted closer and lifted her chin with his hooked finger, drew her gaze to his lips. She really liked his mouth. The shape of it, the thickness of his lips, the way he licked his bottom one sometimes when he was nervous and didn't want anyone to know. "You said someday. Is surgery an option?"

Emma shook her head. "I have sensorineural hearing loss. Both of my inner ears are malformed. This is the best I get as a human."

"As a human," he repeated. "Is that why you wanted to pledge to Kane's Crew? Are you going for a shifter bite?"

"No. A bite won't cure me. I was born with malformed pieces, Dustin. Maybe an animal would improve it, maybe it would make it where I could hear some without my hearing aids, but there is only one thing that will fix me."

Dustin angled his face, frowned, and dropped his finger from her chin. And then suddenly, his eyebrows jacked up in an ah-ha expression. "You mean you're going vamp?"

"I'm taking a break from my coven because I wanted to see life outside of it, you know? My parents wanted that for me, too. But since I was a kid, all I've wanted is to be Turned and be whole."

Dustin gritted his teeth and shook his head at the river. "You are whole."

"You know what I mean."

"No, I don't! You think being a bloodsucker is a fix, Emma? It's not a fucking fix. You're giving up sunlight, food, humanity—"

"Stop!" She shoved him hard. "Stop talking about things you don't understand."

"You don't need to be fixed."

Emma's eyes rimmed with tears, and she ripped her gaze away from him so he wouldn't see how much this hurt. "You don't know what it's like."

"To be different? Fuckin' *false*, Emma. You know what percentage of the population of werewolves are submissive? Do you? Almost zero percent. I grew up the cull pup. I grew up being the disappointment, only supporting my brother's rise to alpha like a fucking servant because he was the important one. I got pitied looks from every wolf I ever met because it must be awful to be me, right?"

"But being submissive isn't a disability!"

"To you!" Dustin stood and walked to the water's edge, ran his hands through his hair, then paced back to her. "Even if I could change the parts I hate about myself, I'd never turn vamp to do it. You won't be *you* anymore. You won't. And now you're pushing for this crew you plan on leaving anyway?"

"Turning vamp isn't an option for you, *wolf*, and I don't have to leave the crew. I would just live on a different schedule."

"For eternity."

"Vampires don't live forever."

"Chhhh. Fucking technicalities now? A couple thousand years in darkness, close enough. You'll watch everyone you love die. You'll watch the crew die of old age, and I'm calling it now—you're going to find a man you love, who dies on you, and you'll carry that hurt for two thousand fucking years. Turning vamp isn't a fix for anything. It's replacing one problem for a dozen more."

"One problem," she repeated, standing. She clenched her hands. "I'm a song-writer, Dustin."

"What?"

"Yeah, that's my passion. I write songs. Some of them are big. Some of them you've probably heard on the radio. I'm a natural," she said, the words tasting bitter against her tongue. "A music prodigy, my teachers said, *if not for the hearing loss*. And I want to write songs for me. Can't you try to understand? My whole heart is full of music, all the time, and I have this voice I can't control, can't stand the sound of, can't hear well enough to hold a tune. So yeah, if I have to give up sunlight and live the exact way I've been raised my whole entire life, which isn't the awful experience you imagine, then yeah, I'll give up steak and sleep during the day."

"Then what are you waiting for? Huh?" Dustin's eyes flashed with anger. "Why are you here trying to be a Blackwing instead of shacking up with your beloved coven and getting your throat ripped out by one of your loving parents?" Dustin was shaking, but she didn't understand why.

"Why are you so offended by this? If you were really my friend, you would at least try to see it from my point of view."

Dustin snarled deep in his throat, and his words came out too gravelly. "I'm a fucking werewolf, Emma. Have you not heard anything about us? You really live in the supe world and don't see what is standing right in front of you? You think you befriended a werewolf, really? Friendship isn't our gig. Blind loyalty to our alphas is. That's it. There's no room for humans or vamps." Dustin stepped up to her and curled his hand around her throat like he wanted to squeeze, but he didn't. His eyes flashed those bright colors, and then he strode off toward the woods, removing his shirt as he went.

"What about the food?"

Dustin turned and walked backward, his face snarled up and terrifying. "Eat it all. Enjoy, Emma.

You'll be on a boring-ass blood diet soon enough."

And then he shoved his jeans down to his ankles and Changed into his black-furred massive wolf before he was even done undressing.

Emma sat heavily on the blanket as the tears that had brimmed in her eyes trickled onto her cheeks. She'd never seen him like that. Never seen him open up about his hate for being submissive or his disgust for vampires. Her heart felt like it had been severed from her body, but why? It was just Dustin, and this shouldn't be a surprise. He was right. Werewolves were psychopaths at best, and she'd been mistaken to think he was different.

The haunting note of a howl lifted on the wind, rising and rising, and she closed her eyes against the world and just listened to his song.

Dustin's howl was the saddest, most beautiful sound she'd ever heard.

SIX

Emma wiped her cheeks with the back of her hand and lifted Dustin's shirt from the pile of wild grass where he'd discarded it. She folded it and then checked the tree line before she lifted it to her nose and smelled the fabric. It smelled like cologne and Dustin. So good.

What if he was watching her from the shadows? The hair lifted on the back of her neck as she hurried to pick up his jeans. Movement on the edge of the woods caught her attention, and there he was, human, naked, muscles rippling as he strode directly for her. His eyes were still glowing blue and green, and his mouth was set in a grim line that said he wasn't through with his tirade yet. Shit.

She clutched his clothes to her chest and readied to strip him down right back. Testy werewolf, judging her life choices—and whoa, he wasn't stopping. Back up! Dustin was coming in hot!

Eyes sparking with intensity, he cupped her neck and pulled her to him. His lips crashed onto hers, shocking her completely. He pushed his tongue past her lips, forced his way into her mouth, and hell balls, a post-Change, riled up, oversexed Dustin was hot. He ripped his clothes from her arms and threw them away, then gripped her waist hard, dragging her against him.

"I'm sorry," he growled against her lips.

An apology from a werewolf? Maybe she had been right about Dustin after all. Perhaps he was different.

He gripped the back of her hair, not too tight, not too gently...just perfect to get her revved up. With a soft moan, she slipped her arms around his neck and allowed him to lift her off the ground. She thought he would get rough in his hurry to get to the blanket, but he didn't. He cradled her in his arms as if she weighed nothing at all, working her lips with gentle sucks and nips. Overwhelmed with feelings she didn't understand, Emma pecked his lips, then buried her face against his neck, inhaled deeply. He smelled of fur.

Dustin must not have minded the affection right in the middle of their kiss since he rested his jaw on her forehead and sighed a relieved sound. Then, and only then, did he carry her slowly to the blanket, keeping his gait smooth and steady.

He laid her down as though she was fragile. As though she was a flower with thin petals. Trailing a finger down her tear-stained cheeks, he shook his head, his eyes filling with regret. He opened his mouth, then closed it again, and she got it. Words were hard for her now, too. She didn't like fighting with Dustin. Didn't like arguing. Didn't like upsetting him. She drew his hand to her lips and kissed his palm. He watched her lay kisses along his wrist, up to the inside crease of his elbow.

Inhaling deeply, he pulled the hem of her silk blouse until it slid over her hair, and then he cradled the back of her head and laid her down gently. Emma wanted to laugh and cry and grin and cry some more. Dustin was capable of great gentleness—something she would've never guessed in a million years. Oh, this man didn't know it, but his tenderness right now, right when she needed it, was earning her devotion.

His triceps was flexed as he locked one arm by her head, and with his other hand, he unclasped the front fasten of her bra and pushed it aside. He blew out a shaky breath as he drew his touch lightly around one of her breasts, raising gooseflesh where his heat met her skin.

"The first time I saw you," he murmured, speaking carefully, "I thought you were beautiful. I thought something was wrong with me because there were two shifter females right there, right near me, and I couldn't keep my attention off the human."

"You did not," she said low.

Dustin dipped down and sipped her lips, then rested his forehead against hers. His hair tickled her cheeks, so she tucked it behind his ears.

"You wore a blue shirt, no logo, hugged your curves. Dark blue jeans with holes at the knees, and your hair was down in waves. When the sun peeked out from the clouds, it made your hair look like it had gold streaks. Your eyes looked so green with Kane's woods behind you. I thought you would be sweet. Too sweet, but then when you flipped me off and turned off one of your hearing aids, my wolf sat up straight inside me and couldn't stop watching you." He kissed the base of her throat. "Little human who knew how to posture. Who knew how to handle herself in the middle of all those monsters." He kissed her right under her earlobe. "You were writing in that journal, and I wanted to see just one page, so bad. I wanted to see what you were writing, and if it was about me. I hoped it was about me, even though we were strangers. But every time I got too close, you closed it up and lifted your little chin. You glared me down like I wasn't scary to you. I knew you wouldn't let me push you around, and my wolf sat up a little straighter." He kissed her lips, nibbled her bottom one. "Remember when I bought all that Chinese food and the D-Team sat around eating, waiting on the call-backs from Kane?"

"Yes," she panted out.

"I bought the food for you. I wanted you to eat with me, and you did. And then I wanted you to eat after me. I wanted your lips to touch what mine did. I couldn't stop watching you. And still, you didn't take my shit. You saw through it. You giggled when the others wanted to murder me. And my wolf sat up a little straighter."

Was this what it was like to fall in love? Emma ran her knuckles along the underneath of his defined jaw. "What else?" she whispered.

He smiled and bit her wrist gently. Emma gasped and rolled her hips in an embarrassing reaction. Dustin didn't seem to mind, though. His eyes turned wicked, and he sucked hard right where his teeth had been.

"Remember when my arm got dislocated at the stables?"

She dipped her chin once. His hand was tracing her body, curve by curve, and it was harder to focus now.

"I was going to bite Winter. I couldn't help it. I was hurting and she was snarling, riled up, calling my animal out to battle, and then you came running over. I couldn't stop watching you as you instructed her how to put my shoulder back in its socket. My wolf, at the peak of wanting to attack, just...stopped...to watch you."

"Has this happened to you before?" she asked, risking it all. Risking this moment for an answer she wished for more than anything.

Dustin shook his head slowly. "Never. You're terrifying. You're a hellion. You're fragile and outspoken and flawless."

"Even hearing impaired?" she whispered.

Dustin leaned down and kissed her again, then rested his cheek on hers and said against her ear, "I'll hear for the both of us. You're perfect to me, Emma. Human or vampire, I'll still be your friend."

And that right there—that was exactly what she needed after their fight. He was accepting her no matter what. She didn't know how he'd done it, but Dustin had seduced her mind, body, and soul. He'd bound them in ways he probably didn't understand. He'd changed the way she thought about werewolves, about the crew, about people, about men, about everything.

Emma reached down and unbuttoned her jeans. Dustin frowned and looked down at where he was pressed between her legs.

"Emma," he said in a tone that said he was denying her.

"I'm on birth control," she whispered, pushing her pants down her hips.

He shook his head back and forth, back and

forth, as his breath deepened and his eyes turned bright like blue and green flames. "That's…" He swallowed hard. "That's not like kissing in the woods, Emma. Sex will change things."

"For the better?"

"I don't know. There are things I haven't told you about me. About why I'm here…"

Emma pressed one hand over the angel wing on his chest. "But you will, right?"

His nostrils flared as she brushed her fingers down to his erection. "Yes. Eventually."

Good enough. She wasn't surprised at all that Dustin was slow at exposing secrets. He'd hidden how affected he was by her this entire time. She'd had no idea, and now she was fine with being patient because some deep instinct told her *Dustin is worth it*. "That's good enough for me now."

There was a loaded moment where they locked eyes, and the air sparked between them with something just above her senses. Some animal magnetism or…something.

Dustin slid his hands between her legs and dragged his fingers up her wet folds as he kissed her again. She let off a helpless noise and rolled her hips against his hand. Dustin smiled against her lips, then nipped her with a growl.

Needing to explore his body, she ran her fingertips over the swell of muscle on his shoulders, his biceps, and forearms, then back up to his chest. Down, down his chiseled abs and lower. As she gripped his shaft, the growl in his throat got loud enough for her to hear, not just feel. He bucked into the hold she made with her hand, and his kisses suddenly got harder, more urgent.

His lips drifted to her neck, and he sucked hard enough to sting, then grazed his teeth against her sensitive skin. Tease. He wouldn't bite her, surely, but just in case…

"Don't bite me, okay?"

"Someday you'll beg me for it," he said in a low voice she almost didn't recognize. "I'll wait for you to ask." The promises of a werewolf. *I'll only bleed you when you beg.* Dustin didn't understand humans. Pain wasn't sexy, and she was nobody's prey.

Dustin rocked forward in her hands. He was so close to her entrance, brushing into her shallowly. Emma released him, and when he slid deep inside her, she gasped, arched back. So big. Almost too big.

Relax. So good anyway, but she hadn't been ready for him to stretch her like that. Dustin eased out of her slowly, then bucked into her again. She was ready this time.

Cradling her head, he buried his face against her neck and pushed into her again, bumping her clit just right at the peak of each thrust. God, he was good. Perfect pace, perfect biting kisses on her throat, perfect body against hers. So strong, so snarly, so sexy. His lips were back on hers again, and as he pushed into her, he groaned a soft sound into her mouth. Well, fuck it all, she was gone now, clawing at him desperately while he built the pressure between her legs to blinding.

She bit his lip hard and then arched back against the blanket when he worked his lips over her collar bone. So close. The stars were so bright. His lips were urgent on her breast now, and she dug her nails into his back desperately. Stars, stars, blinding. Stars in the woods. In the woods? She was looking at the trees upside down. Four stars. Eyes? No…

"Aah," Dustin groaned out, bucking into her faster. He was close, too, and that was a good thing because she couldn't hold her release back any longer.

Orgasm blasted through her, and she curled around the sensation, clung to his strong shoulders. Dustin slammed into her and hesitated. Warmth shot into her, and when he pulled back and rammed into her again, she could feel him emptying himself deep within her. So. Damn. Sexy.

They crashed against each other like two storms colliding. She couldn't believe how good this felt, how deeply satisfying every drive of his dick was. Sex had never been like this, not with anyone.

Dustin gritted his teeth. His chest wasn't rattling anymore with his growl, and he settled against her, laid his full weight on top. He was much bigger than her, but it wasn't uncomfortable.

"Are you okay?" he asked.

What a strange question. Of course, she was okay. "You make me feel safe," she said, too loud in the dark. She winced, but Dustin eased up and smiled down at her. "Say that again."

Pleasure heated her cheeks, and she ducked her gaze. In a softer voice, she said, "You make me feel safe, Dustin."

He exhaled a long breath, and when she looked

back up at him, he had his eyes closed and a sweet smile curving his lips. "No one's ever said that about me before." His grin stretched wider. "You owe the compliment jar."

Emma laughed and rolled her eyes upward. The stars in the woods were gone. Maybe they'd been lightning bugs.

"What?" he asked, stroking her hair away from her face.

"Nothing. Everything is perfect."

Dustin traced her lips with the tip of his finger. "I like this smile on you. It's my new favorite."

"What was your old favorite?"

"The one you get when you think I'm funny. The one you give when everyone else is annoyed at me."

"Well, you're horribly annoying."

"Fucking tell me about it. I think Beast has choked me a dozen times."

She cracked up because that was actually a really accurate number. "Yeah, you never learn your lesson with him and Logan. They're going to lose their minds and kill you someday."

"Nah, I'm safe enough with them."

The smile slipped from her face, and she played

with the ends of his sandy-blond hair. "What makes you so confident? They feel like monsters to me, and I'm human."

"It's the one advantage to being submissive. Dominants think twice before killing you. It's instinct. Their animals tell them to protect shifters like me."

Slowly, Emma moved his hair back and traced the scars on his neck. "Your brother doesn't have that instinct, and he's dominant."

Dustin's smile faded in an instant, and he rolled off her. Not away though, just beside her, where he rested his hands on his stomach and sighed up at the night sky. "It's complicated with him. He's sick right now, but he'll get better, and this stuff won't happen as much anymore. He'll be able to stop himself."

"What's wrong with him?"

Dustin rolled his head back and forth on the blanket denying her an answer.

"There's a vampire in my coven, Lorren. He's very old, even though he looks like he is my age. He's losing his mind, getting dangerous. The coven calls it The Sickening. Is it like that?"

Dustin rolled toward her and traced a line from between her breasts down her stomach to her belly-button. He wouldn't meet her eyes. "My brother's sickness is caused by the need for vengeance. Vengeance is poison for werewolves. It rots them from the inside out. People think we are just bad. Genetics, or bad wolves breeding bad wolves. The truth is the animals are to blame. Too many dominants, not enough submissives. It's like a mob. One or two people get riled up about something, and that energy breeds more violent energy. Werewolves get caught in the energy, and their animals make it impossible to escape."

"But not you."

"No, not me."

"Because you're different."

He bore his teeth in a flash. She could feel his snarl all the way through his fingertips when he dragged his touch across her hip. "Being different isn't good for a wolf, Emma. Being different will get me killed someday. Early. There's nothing I can do but draw my life out as long as I can. For a wolf like me, a broken one, my life invited pain from my first shift to now, any time I encountered one of my kind. It's not like with Logan or Beast, or even Kane. Werewolves don't have an instinct to protect me.

There is instinct to remind me of my place at the bottom of the pack. And the way to remind me...is to bleed me."

"But you aren't in the pack anymore."

Dustin frowned and didn't answer. Instead, he sat up, cradled her in his arms, and pushed up. He strode with her toward the water.

"Hell no, it's cold!"

Dustin stopped in a flash. "Shit. I forgot you're human. You have chilly bumps."

She snickered and wrapped her arms around her middle to try and keep some warmth there. "Chilly bumps?"

"That's what my mom called them." Dustin walked her back to the blanket and dressed her like she was an incapable toddler, all the while wearing such a serious expression.

"I'm not going to die because of a little cold weather you know," she said, amused.

"You could catch a cold."

"And take some cold medicine."

"Or pneumonia. I heard that's a serious thing." He shoved the bags of cold food off the blanket and wrapped it around her until only her eyeballs showed.

"Oh my gosh, you are ridiculous."

Dustin stood there, hands on his hips, surveying his work. With a satisfied nod, he grabbed his clothes and the food and said magnanimously, "You may eat in my car, with the heat on full-blast. I'm probably going to melt, but fuck it. You let me put my dick in your—"

"Okay, that's good. Let's not suck out all the romance from our night, shall we?"

"Right." He led her in the direction of the parking lot. "You hump very nicely and diligently. Compliment jar, you owe me a blow job."

"That's not how it is supposed to work, and furthermore, that's one of the pros of being a future vampire. No blow jobs."

"Oh, because of your future fangs?" Dustin scrunched up his face. "Okay point for that one. Con, no reflection in the mirror, so how are you supposed to put on make-up or trim your pubes?"

Emma laughed so loud her abs hurt. "Why are you using a mirror for that? Just look down, dumbass. And they have vampire mirrors now. You just flip a little switch, and it casts this special light so vampires can see themselves. They even invented some vampire app for phones so we can take selfies. Hiss, hiss."

"Also con, you won't have a soul anymore."

"Says who?"

"Says everyone."

Emma rolled her eyes. Her parents were the nicest people she knew. They definitely had souls. "Pro, I'll be able to fly, shift into this crazy powerful ball of bats, and get really strong. Also pro, my boobs will stay perky for thousands of years."

But Dustin had stopped and was looking behind them now with narrowed eyes, so she halted her penguin waddle. "What's wrong?"

Dustin's nostril's flared slightly as he inhaled, and now his eyes were glowing so brightly they were hard to look at. He stood frozen like a stone, his attention on the woods behind them, but when Emma looked, she didn't see or sense anything.

Dustin said something too low for her to understand, so she frowned at his lips and waited. He didn't repeat it, though. Instead, he pressed his hand on her lower back and guided her in front of him, hurrying her toward the parking lot, his attention never wavering from something behind them.

Now she had real chilly bumps. If his wolf senses were all riled up, then something was wrong. She opened the front of the blanket so she could walk faster, but her high heels still kept her from sprinting. And anyway, when she tried, Dustin pulled her back and told her, "Slow. Don't run."

"Are we being hunted?" That was the only thing that made sense right now. Why else wasn't she allowed to give into her instincts to flee and bolt from this place?

"I don't know." His voice sounded odd. A lie?

"By an animal or shifter."

He didn't answer.

"Dustin!"

"I don't know!" but his voice still sounded weird. Off, just a little.

By the time they reached the car, she was panting in fear. As he helped her inside, there was this awful feeling that something bad would happen to Dustin while he was running around the back of the car to get in. She shoved his door open to save him a precious millisecond.

Dustin jammed the key into the ignition and

turned over the engine, shifted into reverse, and peeled out of the spot. And before he was even stopped, he had it shifted into first and was gunning it out of the dark and empty parking lot. The clouds had covered the moon and all the stars so it was dark outside the window.

"Everything is fine," Dustin said loudly over the roar of the engine as he switched to second gear. "I was just being careful."

"Bullshit," she called him out.

His teeth were clenched tightly, and he kept checking the rearview mirror. Another secret Dustin wanted to keep. Add it to the pile.

She huffed a breath and ripped her gaze away from him to stare out the window.

But as she watched the dark woods blurring by, she could've sworn she saw something massive running parallel to the road, way off in the trees. Something monstrous.

And then she heard it—the long call of a wolf.

Only there were no wild wolves here.

Dustin was panting hard, exposing his neck. To her? She was human and no threat to him. Another long wolf howl filled the air.

"Fuck," Dustin gritted out as though in pain.

And because she was desperate to end whatever was happening to him, she leaned over and pressed a kiss against his bicep. "It's okay. I'm here. Everything is fine. We just need to get out of hearing range. Foot on the gas, one mile at a time. It's me and you."

Dustin's abs flexed like he wanted to retch, but he was nodding now. Emma turned up the volume of the radio until he hunched against the sound. Stroking his hair back so she could see more of his face, she leaned forward and pressed her lips against his neck, right over his tripping pulse. She sucked gently, then grazed his skin with her teeth. His body began to relax, and his breath came easier.

And as the howls faded behind them, she rested her cheek against his shoulder and asked, "Is that your old pack?"

Dustin shook his head and ran a hand down his facial scruff. "No, Emma. That's my current pack."

SEVEN

His current pack? That was a weird way of putting it, but when she'd asked him, Dustin had shut down on her. He'd stared out the front window the entire way to the bar, never once casting a single glance her way on the twenty-minute drive.

Clearly, Dustin was freaking out by whatever dynamics were in his pack, so as he coasted along the winding road, Emma pulled a cold burger out of the bag and began eating it. She fed him a bite every time she took one, and little by little, he softened his grip on the steering wheel.

"This car looks hella expensive," she said around a bite.

"It was."

"Are you a millionaire?"

"Ha!" He still looked white as a sheet, but at least he was smiling again. "Typical. Interested in my money."

"Please, I don't need your money. I have money invested and in savings."

"Then why were you going on about how you need to get a job so you can afford your motel room, hmmm?"

"Because I'm not touching my investments or savings! I want to be a rich vampire. I invest almost all of my song-writing money and pay for my living with regular jobs. Was that your brother back there?"

"Yes."

"Why was he calling you?"

"I don't know. Do you want to go back and ask him?"

"Hell no, that was scary. There's Logan's truck," she said, pointing to the parking lot in front of Drat's Boozehouse. "French fry?" She flopped a soft one beside his cheek and waited for him to turn and bite it out of her hand. "So, what do we tell the D-Team?"

"About what?"

"About us."

"Nothing, it's none of their damn business."

"Fine, but you have to be nice to me in there."

"I'm always nice." He said that with a wicked smile. "If you want me to eat you out in the bathroom, give me a signal."

She cracked a grin and played along. "What kind of signal?"

"I don't know. Do some of that sign language stuff." He made a hole with one hand and stuck his other finger in the middle a few times. "Do that if you get horny. It'll be my bat signal."

"You're exhausting."

He turned the music down, then said, "Thank you," and gave her a megawatt grin that would've buckled her knees if she were standing. Dustin was trouble in a pretty package, for sure and for certain.

Whatever he was feeling back there with his old pack was dissipating by the second. And really, a part of her was relieved to be this close to the D-Team again. They were a mixed bag of nuts, but they had built some strange thread of loyalty to each other during this crew interview process. She was at least fifty-four percent certain they would have his back if Dustin's old pack moseyed on in here. Geez, no wonder he wanted to pledge to Kane's Crew. His brother was a grade-A asshole, and the way he talked about the others always putting him in his place, she was pretty sure she hated every douchebag in his old pack. And that was saying something because she hated very little in her life.

"I like your sex hair," Dustin said through a cheeky grin as she got out.

Emma looked at her reflection in the window and nearly choked on air. She looked like a lion on a bad hair day. And was that…? Was that a leaf? She plucked a twig out of her hair and laughed.

"Wait, I want to keep that." He snatched it from her hand before she could throw it on the ground.

"Why?" she asked as she pulled her crazy hair into a high ponytail.

"Memories. That was our first bang, Shortcake. That's a pretty big fuckin' deal."

"Please, like you haven't been with a hundred other women."

"Yeah, but none of them got twigs stuck in their hair." Laughing like he was God's gift to humor, Dustin ducked away from her swat.

She thought he was joking, but he really shoved

the little limb into his back pocket and then crooked his elbow out gallantly. "For the show," he announced.

"Oh, so we *are* a pretend couple tonight?"

"Why not?" he said recklessly.

Oh, that man had the devil in his smile. Emma loved it when he was like this, easy with her, eyes only on her, a real smile on his lips. Perfect hair tumbling down his cheeks, that skin-tight sweater all stuck to his muscles like he was walking the stage in some wet T-shirt contest, and his jeans sitting low on his hips. And his eyes...one green and one blue, and a part of her hoped that was genetic because if she ever had a baby, she would love one with bi-colored eyes, just like Dustin.

Babies? That had come out of nowhere. She needed to rein it in. This was just pretend, and she was getting lost in fantasies of playing house. Dustin had about a hundred too many secrets for her head to be on future babies. Besides, she would be a vampire within the next couple of years, and she'd seen the children of vampire/shifter couples—terrifying little critters with little control.

Dustin held open the door to Drat's for her,

waited for her to pass, and followed shortly, fingertips on her lower back. "D-Team!" he called across the dark-wood bar with the old, rusty street signs decorating most of the walls.

Beast, Logan, and Winter turned around from where they sat at the bar. Aaand so did Kane and Rowan.

"Shit, abort mission," Dustin said, turning her toward the door.

"Bad dog," Emma said as she kept turning them in a full circle until they were facing the bar again. "You need to hang out with Kane and make amends, or we'll never get in the crew. Buy him a drink and kiss his butt."

"I don't know what dragons drink. Arsenic and people's souls?"

"I can hear you," Kane called in a bland voice. He still looked at Dustin like he wanted to burn him to ashes and eat him.

"He hates me," Dustin muttered as they walked toward the bar.

Emma patted his arm. "No, he doesn't."

"Yes, I do," Kane called.

Tonight was going to be awesome.

"If he tries to kill me, do that signature move of yours," Dustin said.

"What move?"

"You know, the one where you knee grown men in the ball sacks."

Emma giggled and shook her head. She had done that once to Dustin. She felt bad about it now, but at the time she thought he was trying to hurt her instead of help her. "I'll protect you."

"Good." Dustin growled at Beast and lunged at him.

The titan didn't move, but only arched one blond brow and looked bored. "You smell like sex."

"Beast!" Emma reprimanded him.

"What?" Beast asked with a deep frown. "Did you do it by the river?"

"Oh, my gosh, were you there?" Emma asked loudly as heat blasted into her cheeks.

"No. That's where Dustin always goes when he's pissed or confused."

"Wait, what?" Dustin asked.

Dustin was talking too quietly, and the noises from the busy bar were confusing her, so Emma diverted to reading lips.

"How do you know where I go?" Dustin asked, shifting his weight from side to side and looking decidedly uncomfortable. His eyes were glowing again.

"I like to stalk things," Beast said nonchalantly, then downed a shot of amber liquor neatly. "You're fun to follow. You don't pay attention, get lost in your head. Gonna get yourself killed."

"Newsflash, psycho, it's not supposed to be fun to stalk people. Stop following me."

"Don't worry, dog." Beast's bright blue eyes narrowed to slits. "I'll keep your secrets on one condition."

"What secrets?" Winter asked.

"Yeah, what secrets," Kane growled out.

Dustin crossed his arms over his chest. "What condition?"

Beast jerked his chin to Emma. "Don't hurt the human." Beast's eyes blazed gold, and his voice dipped to a snarl. "Hurt Emma—"

"Yeah, yeah, and you'll kill me. Take a number." Dustin pointed at Kane. "He wants to kill me." He dragged his finger to Logan. "Also threatens to kill me every day." Dustin snarled at Beast. "You aren't the first or the last to make the threat, werepussy, and I'm still breathing. Emma isn't your concern. And I'm serious, Beast, stop fucking following me." Dustin brushed past Emma without meeting her gaze. "I'm going to take a piss."

EIGHT

Dustin rinsed the soap off his hands and yanked a paper towel from the dispenser. Fuck! Beast had seen him with the pack, heard God knew what, and now he had something to hold over his head. He was too deep into this. Any second this could all blow up in his face, and it wasn't just him who would be hurt now. Emma was right in the line of fire because of his stupid suggestion to pretend to pair up. This was supposed to be make-believe, but today it had felt like the most real part of his life.

Being with her made him happy.

Jesus. Happy? What did that word even mean? It sure as hell didn't exist for werewolves, and especially not one like him.

But still...today had been incredible. She'd kept his mind off Axton and the pack, kept his mind off everything but her, really. Dangerous little creature, that Emma. He needed to keep it together because he was walking a very fine line. Death by the Valdoro Pack or death by the Blackwing Crew. Wolf or Dragon, either death would hurt. And now he would be leaving Emma behind. Something about that thought made his wolf revolt inside of him. Dustin growled and slammed his back against the tile bathroom wall, then slid down to a crouching position and gripped the back of his head. He had to stay human. No more running from the reality of the position he was in by Changing into the wolf. He'd done that tonight with Emma. Got mad, Changed, left her alone in the damn woods where Axton and Jace were. And what could he have done if they'd decided to attack her then? He was bottom rank and submissive. Could he have defended her? Shit, he didn't even know that answer.

She would be on their radar now unless he convinced them it was all a ploy to get into the crew like they'd planned. Maybe if they thought Emma didn't mean anything to him and she was just his ticket into the crew, they would leave her alone.

What was he doing?

He was in way over his head, getting pulled under crashing waves, and what had he done? Grabbed onto Emma's ankle so he could drag her down into the darkness with him. Selfish. Typical werewolf shit, and he hated that he'd put her in danger.

But...

He'd never felt like this. Like maybe everything would be okay somehow. It was nice to have her at his back, finishing his sentences, thinking along the same winding lines he did, smiling at the same stuff he found funny. So beautiful. She would make pretty pups. Girl pups. Ones that looked like her with long curls and big green eyes. He could be a good dad if he had someone like Emma keeping him from fucking everything up. *Ours.*

That felt right.

The door swung open and in walked trouble. Petite Emma, with those sexy curves shoved into tight jeans and that little spaghetti-strap silk shirt. Make-up on point, fresh lip gloss, hair pulled back in a ponytail that gave him a boner on account of it being a beautiful mess, just like his Emma. He'd gotten her hair all ratted like that. She'd let him inside of her. Not like with the other girls she'd mentioned. They were all fucks he *needed* when pack life got too hard or his wolf became unmanageable.

Sex with Emma was different. It was better.

"Why are you staring at my vagina?" she asked. Her voice was thick and a little slurred, but he'd meant it when he'd told Emma her voice was perfect. No other girl he'd ever met sounded like her. He would recognize the tone of her voice from across a busy street.

Dustin cleared his throat and ripped his gaze away from the zipper of her jeans. "Are you here to blow me?"

Emma snorted and knelt down in front of him. "No. You didn't do the bat signal." She shoved her finger a couple of times into a hole she made with her other hand.

Dustin wanted to hold onto his worry for a little while longer, but it was impossible with his dainty little human making lewd gestures like that.

The smile dipped from her lips. "You okay?"

"Fine. Why?"

"You're on the floor like your world just ended."

Dustin took stock of his body. Crap, she was seeing him in a really vulnerable position. "Just dealing with some wolf shit. I'm good."

Emma canted her head, and her delicate eyebrows went into the cutest fucking frown he'd ever seen, right before she scooted between his legs and hugged his waist. She rested her head against his shoulder and sighed. "I bought you a drink. It's something called a Pink Panty Dropper, and it has extra maraschino cherries and a purple umbrella."

Dustin snorted a laugh. "You better not have."

"I roofied it so I can seduce you easier," she murmured, but there was a smile in her voice.

"The girl of my dreams," he muttered. He said it like a joke, but underneath the tease, he absolutely meant it. Emma was flawless.

He inhaled deeply and wrapped his arms around her shoulders. "You really do smell like sex. That's a compliment."

"Well, it's a terrible compliment."

"Thank you."

She shook her head against his shoulder, and he imagined her rolling her eyes. She did that a lot, but with a smile that said she wasn't that annoyed with him.

The door swung open, and Winter stumbled in with a pair of pink girly drinks in her hands and her eyes closed tightly. She was wobbling on her heels and smelled like a brewery. "Stop fooling around. I have to talk to y'all." Winter cracked an eye open and sighed with relief. Then she leaned against the wall beside them and slid down, landing a little too hard. Some of her drink spilled on the dingy tile floor.

"Sloppy drinker," Dustin accused.

Winter responded by handing him the drink, which had, in fact, five maraschino cherries sitting in the bottom and a purple miniature umbrella.

Emma was cracking up at herself.

"You're the worst," he muttered, but he took the horrid drink like a shot, because manners. Werewolves sometimes had them.

Logan kicked open the door and came in holding two more pink drinks and looking pissed. "She fucking ordered them for everyone." He sat down beside Winter with the grumpiest frown on his face.

Dustin snorted, and now Emma was really laughing in his arms, shoulders shaking. God he loved her.

Beast came in four seconds later with two more girl-drinks. He smelled angry. And like maraschino cherries. And last but not least to this bathroom party were Kane and Rowan. How many monsters could they fit in one tiny bathroom? Here was the answer.

Beast handed Kane the fruity drinks and stumbled over to the urinals on the wall. A jingle of his belt and the rip of his zipper, his back to them, Beast started pissing.

"Dude," Logan growled. "There are girls in here."

"Girls pee, too," Rowan slurred.

"How much have you had to drink?" Dustin asked the crowd.

"Enough," Kane muttered, as he sat on Dustin's other side and handed him another pink drink.

"Hard pass," Dustin said.

"Fucking drink it. I'm going to puke if I have to drink both."

Dustin growled but chugged the nasty drink as Rowan settled on the other side of Kane. He felt heavy and terrifying so Dustin shifted his weight toward Winter so he wouldn't barf at the raw dominance wafting from the dragon.

With a snarl, Logan leaned over his mate and shoved Dustin's head. "Back off. Mine."

"I strongly dislike all of you," Dustin groused. "Not you Emma. You're pretty and let me have sex with you, and Winter, you're only annoying in the mornings."

"I second that," Beast said, turning from his piddle-session. "Fuck mornings."

"Did you know public restrooms are one of the filthiest places in the world?" Winter asked. "I read that somewhere."

Emma was slurping out of Kane's remaining drink in his hand while the alpha sucked on his mate's neck. Tonight was weird.

No. As Winter chattered on with the most useless facts on the planet and Beast agreed with everything as he washed his hands, while Kane and Rowan sucked face, and Emma hugged him closer, Dustin thought maybe tonight wasn't weird, but perfect instead. The perfect follow-up to the fear that his pack would catch up to them and hurt Emma.

Sure, the Blackwing Crew would eventually find him out and probably kill him in some torturous way, but for now, they felt a lot safer than the pack. *Safe*.

He huffed a breath and massaged the back of Emma's head.

Safe was just a word, and words meant nothing.

But for Emma?

Dustin frowned down at her. She finished off Kane's drink with a loud slurp. She smiled up at him and looked so proud and so naughty. Yeah, she was safe. She had to be. He would make sure of it. He didn't know how, but he was going to get her out of the trouble that clung to him like a second skin. He would bring hell to earth to make sure no one hurt his little human. She was his to protect, and this was the moment he accepted it. Accepted that she was his priority, that her breaths were more important than his, that her heartbeat was more vital to him than his own. It was the moment he made a silent oath to go to war for her, no matter what it cost him. Because she had to be okay. If Emma existed on this earth, Dustin could believe in goodness.

She poked both corners of his lips with her forefingers and shoved them up into a smile. When he chuckled, Emma sighed a happy sound.

"Why are we all hanging out in the bathroom?" Winter asked suddenly, looking around like she was confused about how she'd gotten there. Sloppy, sloppy.

"Why wouldn't the Blackwings hang out in a dirty bathroom for their first celebration?" Kane asked blandly. "Seems fitting enough to me."

"Agree," Logan said, lifting his full drink. When the umbrella fell out and fluttered to the ground, he stomped on it like a roach.

Winter's face went all mushy, and she cuddled up to the lunatic like he was cute.

"Wait, the Blackwings?" Emma asked Kane.

"Yeah, you've all been invited now. I mean, you still have to bite this lying asshole to get in." Kane tossed Dustin a hate-filled look. "But you all got the folders."

"Didn't you know we were celebrating as a crew tonight?" Rowan asked from the other side of her mate.

"But Beast hasn't gotten one," Emma pointed out.

Beast slammed a pink drink back and gulped. "I got one the other day."

"What?" Logan asked too loud. "Why didn't you tell us?"

Beast shrugged his massive shoulders. "No one

asked."

Everyone sat frozen in silence, staring at the scar-faced behemoth.

Emma was the first to snort, and Winter and Rowan followed. Their quiet snickers turned to laughter, and even Logan chuckled. Beast looked pissed and crossed his arms as he glared at them. Kane shook his head and sighed the saddest sound, and now Dustin couldn't help laughing either.

"To the worst crew in the world," Dustin toasted them. "To the D-Team."

The others repeated in unison, "To the D-Team."

And then they downed the rest of the girly drinks.

NINE

Emma blew on her newly painted nails and carefully turned the page in the celebrity gossip magazine with the pad of her pointer finger. Why were all the lies about celebrities boring this week? Or maybe not boring, but pretty tame compared to the crazy last few days she'd had.

Three days since the bathroom party at Drat's, and she was falling harder for Dustin every second. Right now, she missed him. He was off on some secret mission he wouldn't tell her about when he left the motel this morning. That man still had way too many secrets.

Her phone buzzed on the bed beside her, and the screen lit up. Her heart jumped into her throat when

Werewolf Megadick came up in the text. He'd programmed the name himself when she wasn't looking and also added a picture of two flies mating, which now popped up every time he texted or called.

Are you in your room?

Carefully, so she didn't ding her brand new red nails, she typed in, *Yes. Come over. I need help.* Send.

There was an immediate knock on the door. "Emma, are you okay?" Dustin yelled, sounding frantic.

"Come in," Emma called.

"The door's locked!"

"Use your key!"

"Oh, yeah." The door lock dinged the entry sound, and he shoved the door open, his eyes glowing. He looked around the room like he was searching for danger.

Emma pointed at her butt. "My nails are wet, and I have a wedgie."

"Are you fucking serious? I thought you were in trouble, and you want me to pick your wedgie?"

She grinned and nodded.

His gaze dipped to her butt where she was only wearing a pair of bikini cut panties with her tank top.

Dustin cleared his throat. "It would be my pleasure."

But when he approached the bed, he flopped onto his belly beside her and pulled the other side of her panties into the wedgie, creating a make-shift thong.

"Dustin," she grumbled, turning the page of the magazine.

He bounced her butt-cheeks like basketballs. "So jiggly. This is the best ever." He gently bit one cheek, and then the other, then went back to wiggling her cheeks even faster.

Emma rolled her eyes and laughed.

"I'm so turned on right now it's ridiculous," he murmured in a husky voice. "Look at my boner."

She glanced over her shoulder to where Dustin had rolled onto his side. Indeed, he was pitching quite the tent with his jeans.

"We should fool around before I show you my surprise," Dustin suggested.

"What surprise?"

"A surprise that will make you want to give me a hundred hand jobs." He settled over her, his hands and knees on either side of her. "I'm going to take off your clothes now."

She laughed and said, "Dustin, my nails are wet."

"Mmm," he said. "I do like the red. I'll take care of you then. You just sit there and wiggle around like a tuna."

"This is not sexy at all."

Dustin pushed her tank top gently up her back, running his hands along her skin as he went. He eased it off of her, careful of her nails, then leaned down and sucked on the back of her neck.

"I take it back," she murmured. "This is really sexy."

He smiled against her skin and nipped her there. He was bitey any time they fooled around, but he had never done it hard enough to break the skin and Turn her. She trusted him now. Trusted him in ways that terrified her.

Dustin lifted off her, and she watched over her shoulder as he took off his shirt. His abs flexed with the movement, and his hair was mussed when his shirt hit the floor. Dustin clenched his jaw once, and his eyes sparked with an intensity that drew a soft gasp from her lips. On his knees, he unbuttoned his jeans and pulled down the zipper.

"I want to feel your skin against mine." He'd said

it too soft to hear, but had formed the words well enough for her to read his lips easily. He did that now, naturally. He probably didn't even realize it, but there had been a huge change in him over the last few days. He automatically turned his face toward her so she could read his lips when he said something he didn't want the others to hear. He even did it when he spoke up.

Dustin shimmied out of his jeans and gracefully laid on her back, pressing his warm chest against her shoulder blades. There were his clever lips again. She arched back and angled her head to give him more access. His hand went around her throat but stayed gentle.

That man spent some serious time working her into a desperate frenzy. He kissed her neck, back, her hips, and then up to her shoulders on an endless loop until she was begging him to stop the torture and make her come. Feverishly, she rolled her hips against the bed where she could get the barest of friction on her clit if she pushed forward enough. Dustin gripped her hip hard, and she gasped when he lifted her waist off the bed. It had happened so fast she was shocked to find herself up on her knees, his head under her, his face right there between her legs. His hands went to her hips, and he pulled her down, closer. The first brush of his tongue on her clit just about did her in.

"Dustin," she moaned.

He was good when she begged. Desperation in her voice always got a reaction from him. Teasing done, he pulled her lower and pushed his tongue into her. Her hips jerked. She tossed her head back and cried out. The next stroke, he pushed into her deeper, then sucked on her clit, then pushed in, sucked. He set a rhythm, but she was already halfway there. She rocked against his face, encouraging him, rushing him faster because she was losing ground. Losing it. Losing all thought. Fuck, he was so good at this.

She cried out every time he pushed into her, and right as she was at the peak of pleasure, right as the first pulse of orgasm was about to burst through her, Dustin shoved her upward and disappeared out from under her. Without missing a beat, he entered her from behind, filled her, and buried himself so deeply inside of her, the orgasm happened despite the interruption.

He was slow and methodical, drawing every

aftershock out of her as she moaned. She thought he would have to thrust into her for a while to get off, but he gritted out her name two strokes later and bucked hard. Warmth spread inside of her in pulsing jets. He didn't go erratic, but kept it steady as he pumped his seed into her. Was she coming again? Her aftershocks were so intense it was a possibility. He leaned forward across her back, pressing his chest against her, and she could feel the rattling growl that didn't quite reach her hearing. And then there was teeth. Teeth, teeth, teeth, almost hard enough to break the skin over her shoulder blade. And a part of her wanted him to do it. A part of her wanted him to claim her and bind them forever in the way shifters chose their mates. A huge piece of her heart already felt like Dustin's mate even though she was human.

He would do it if she asked. He always gave into her begging. All she had to do was murmur, "Do it," and he would sink his teeth into her and change the course of their lives forever. He would give her a wolf. A wolf. A wolf? No. That wasn't the plan. She was going to be a vampire someday. She wanted Dustin, but not a wolf. She wanted to sing. Emma bit her lip hard against the urge to plead with him to claim her.

Dustin released her skin and eased out of her. Warmth flooded between her legs, and with a satisfied sigh, Emma dropped her forehead to the bed. Instinct made her rock back and forth still as her aftershocks pulsed on, lighter and lighter. Sexy Dustin. Sexy wolf. Sexy man. Sexy mate.

His hand was warm on her back as he slid it up her spine. Pulling her hair, he angled her face toward him and kissed her. Drank her more like. Or perhaps she was drinking him. God, she could almost feel his beautiful soul here in the quiet of the room. Quiet. Too quiet.

She messed with her hearing aids but got nothing. Stupid rechargeable batteries needed to be replaced. Gently, Dustin pulled the aids from her ears, one at a time, and dropped them into the charger beside the bed. His face was so beautiful, like an angel, as he pulled her tightly against him. Dustin swallowed hard, frowned down at her lips, his fingers trailing up and down her ribs.

Slowly, he brushed her hair out of her face and lifted his hand into the air. And then he did the most important, most impactful thing a man had ever done for her.

He signed, *Emma, I love you.*

Her face crumpled immediately, and tears spilled from her eyes. Embarrassed, she buried her face against his chest as her shoulders shook with her crying. He didn't rush her, or push her. He simply held her close, cupped the back of her head, and rested his cheek on her hair until she could get control of her emotions again.

Finally, finally, Emma eased back and lifted her hand in front of him, and then slowly, so he could understand it, she signed, *I love you, too.*

TEN

Dustin paced near the door. He should've done it like he planned. Got her flowers and taken her out to eat. Dated her like a human, and then at the end of the night, when he was dropping her off at her motel door, told her he loved her like they did in the three shitty late-night rom-coms he'd forced himself to watch. Emma deserved romance.

Maybe this was okay. Or maybe not. She'd cried after he signed his feelings to her, but he didn't know what that meant. Human women cried about everything, and he had no idea whether those were happy or sad tears. God, he couldn't do this. He couldn't make her happy, so why was he even trying?

Emma turned on the shower in the bathroom,

and Dustin paced again. He ran his hands through his hair out of a nervous habit and bit back a growl. He hadn't said that to anyone. Well, technically he still hadn't said I love you out loud to anyone, but this one counted. He'd built it up in his head so much over the last couple days, from the second he figured out what this devoted feeling was in his gut. Emma was his, and he wanted to make her happy, like she made him happy.

Off-key notes drifted from the bathroom, and he stopped his pacing to listen to her sing. She sounded happy. Maybe Emma didn't need flowers when he made big statements. *Let's bite her.*

"Shut the fuck up, wolf," he muttered.

Quietly, he padded to the bathroom door so he could hear her better over the running shower. She was singing so softly he couldn't make out the words—they all slurred together. Her hearing aids were still in the charger. A smile stretched Dustin's face and felt so good. She'd said it back. He'd been studying American Sign Language relentlessly any hour he spent away from her, but he was only comfortable with the simple alphabet right now. He would learn it all though. It would just take time. And practice. Emma had been having problems with her aids lately. She fiddled with them too much, and they needed to be re-charged all the time. Maybe he should buy her better ones. Were there better ones? He would have to research this.

She was still singing. God, he loved her voice. Because she gave it to him. She would never sing like this if she knew anyone else was in the room, but for him? She couldn't hear herself, but she was still humming. That must mean something, right? That he made her extra happy? Extra comfortable? Dustin's grin got so big it made his face ache.

Dustin pressed his shoulder blades against the door and leaned his head back, closed his eyes to memorize the tone of her voice. There was a fluttering sound that was ruining the moment, though. Dustin opened his eyes and glared at the desk against the wall. Emma's journal was open, and the top page was lifting in the vent breeze.

Dustin was pulled to it like a bug to a light. He'd thought about this journal so much. Obsessed about it, really. He'd wanted to see her thoughts so badly, and here it was, open, calling to him, tempting him. A good man would've closed it and let it be, but Dustin was a werewolf, and his moral compass was a little bent, so he murmured, "Oops," and flipped it open to the middle.

He read the neat handwriting, a few lines of a song. It was a ballad, a lonely one. Dark. Hmm. Dustin locked his arm against the table and turned the page to the next song. After reading that one, he flipped through two more until he came to a drawing of a panther. It was Winter. She was lying in the shadows of a group of white pines, head turned to the side looking straight at him. The drawing was in black ink, but the eyes were colored gold. Damn. Emma was really good at sketching—a true creative, clearly.

There was another song about wanting more. Dustin liked music as much as the next person, but these were clearly written for other people. To sell maybe, he didn't know, but most of the lyrics didn't match what he'd seen of Emma. She was good. The choruses were catchy, and he wished he could hear them with music. Guitar maybe, like the old scratched-up one that sat on a stand in the corner.

But as he continued to flip through, he lingered on the drawings most. After Winter's Panther, there were angel wings, like his tattoos, and then a set of eyes, one green, one blue. Dustin's heart froze in his chest. At the bottom, she'd written, *Who are you?*

Next was a drawing of his black-furred wolf with his teeth bared. That was what he had probably looked like when he and Kane had almost gone to blows at the trailer park. Fucker had forced a Change that hurt so bad. The next was of him in the woods, face turned up at the moon, lips pursed in a howl. It was a dark drawing, done in some medium other than ink. When he smudged the corner, the black strokes smeared. He sniffed his finger. Charcoal or something close.

The next few pages were songs, hopeful ones. Love ballads, as if her entire mood had changed. One talked about seeing the real side of a person. But the next was about a man with too many secrets. Dustin swallowed hard and turned the page. It was a picture of him in his human form, striding from the woods, naked, eyes glowing blue and green, face looking intense. He was reaching out. This must've been how she saw him the night he'd Changed in the woods, but had come back to her, needing to touch her to settle the wolf inside of him. At the bottom, she had written, *I know you're still good.*

The next song was about falling for a man who was too good for her.

Shit.

He didn't want to trick her into thinking he was more than a monster. Here he was sent to betray the Blackwing dragons. And now, if he did what Axton and Jace demanded, he would betray her, too. He wasn't better than her, no. Dustin wasn't worthy of a woman like Emma.

He could never bite her, never give into the urging of his wolf. Love didn't work like that, and he couldn't allow himself to take her chance to sing away, or to tether her to a man who would drag her down into the shadows with him.

Maybe it was a good thing she would turn vamp on him. Then she would be strong and able to defend herself from the trouble that followed him. Maybe then, they would be on the same level, and she could handle his demons. Emma the human was too, vulnerable, easily injured. Emma the vampire, though... She would be a force to be reckoned with. He fucking hated vamps, but he would still love Emma when she Turned.

And she would finally be able to sing all these

songs she'd written.

"What are you doing?" Emma asked from the open doorway of the bathroom.

He didn't jump. Dustin wasn't startled because he'd heard the door open. "Reading your journal," he answered.

She looked upset, but he didn't give her the chance to filet him. He blurred to her and wrapped her up in his arms, rocked her gently side to side. "I get it now, about you wanting to be a vampire."

Emma froze against him, but softened in seconds and slid her hands up his back. "So you aren't mad about it anymore? You won't try to talk me out of it?"

Dustin shook his head.

"Will you stop being my friend if I'm a vampire?" she asked.

The worry in her voice ripped his guts out. Emma eased back, and her forest green eyes were so earnest and full of hope.

"We're past that, Shortcake. Vampire, human, or werepickle, I'll still be your friend. I'll be more if you let me."

"What are you saying?"

Dustin leaned forward and kissed her lips, softly

like she deserved. As he eased away, he murmured, "We're not pretend anymore. Not to me."

She looked mushy and made a high-pitched sound that made him hunch at the pain it caused to his ears.

"Sorry," she said softer, placing her hands over his ears like that would fix it.

He laughed and pulled them away, kissed both of her palms and jerked his head toward the door. "I have surprises for you."

"What surprises?"

A home cooked meal prepared by him. He'd listened when she told him she was tired of fast food. Telling her would ruin the surprise, though, and for the first time in his life, he cared about stuff like that. "You'll see."

"What should I wear to see these surprises?"

He plucked the tucked end of her towel and let the fabric slip to the ground. God, her body was beautiful. "Nothing is good."

"No one would appreciate that but you," she said, still too loud as she gathered the towel back to cover herself. She was so fucking cute when she giggled to herself like this.

And also she was dead wrong. Any red-blooded, heterosexual male would be tripping over his own boner to see Emma naked. She had the perfect curves, full tits, hourglass shape, grab-able ass, and a confidence that made her so damn attractive.

And her skin was so soft he wanted to bite it. *We should.*

Dustin shook his head hard to punish the wolf for such thoughts, cupped her cheeks, and lifted her gaze to his lips. "I'm gonna go load up the car. Come out when you're dressed." He smirked. "Or not dressed, whatever."

Emma shocked him when she suddenly went to her tiptoes and threw her arms around his neck. She rubbed her cheek against his like a happy feline and sighed. On a whim, he lifted her up until she wrapped her legs around him and sat on the bed with her on his lap. And there they sat, rocking back and forth gently, as he stroked her wet hair and hugged her close.

This was the moment his life changed. Oh, he'd been heading here for a while. With his wolf paying attention to her, the kiss in the woods, the easy laughter, the budding affection, sex, and wanting to bite her...the I love yous. Somewhere along the way, he'd begun to change his mind on what was important. No...*Emma* had changed his mind. She'd changed him from the inside out, and now he wanted to be a better man for her. One she could rely on. One who wouldn't hurt her.

This right here was the moment that he decided he couldn't betray the Blackwings.

For Emma, he was going to betray his pack instead.

ELEVEN

Tugging her hoodie over her head, Emma stepped outside and froze at what she saw. The D-Team was all loading up the back of Logan's truck. Dustin's gaze immediately collided with hers as he shoved a giant blue cooler in the back. He gave her a charming wink that made her stomach flutter.

She offered him a smile and wave, then grabbed Winter's arm as she passed. "What's happening?"

Winter grinned big, her smoky gray eyes sparking with excitement. "Tonight is the first trailer park party. Dustin planned it."

"False," Dustin called loud enough for her to hear. "I planned a trailer park party for me and Emma so I could maybe get my dick stroked, but then these assholes begged to tag along. Cock blockers, every one of them."

It was chilly out, so Emma shoved her hands into her pockets and jogged over to him. He turned and caught her up in a back cracking hug like they hadn't just parted ways forty-five minutes ago. He eased his lips near her ear. "Plus I know you like hanging out with these losers, so maybe I invited them a little. Remember the bat signal."

Emma giggled and kissed him hard, bit his bottom lip at the end, hugged his neck as tight as she could and slid back down to the ground. "You're my favorite werewolf."

"Not a compliment. I'm the only werewolf you don't hate."

"Still counts." Emma shrugged coyly and scrambled into the back seat of Logan's truck.

Dustin slid in beside her, scooting her with his hip.

"Whoa, Dustin's not bitching about shotgun?" Logan asked, his dark brows knitted into a frown as he climbed into his truck. "Are you sick? I mean besides in the head."

"I feel fine, fuck you very much." Dustin lifted his

arm over Emma's head and pulled her close. "Sex puts me in a good mood, like a normal person."

"Dustin," Emma reprimanded him.

"What? You don't screw and tell, and that's classy of you. I'm not classy."

Ever the optimist of the crew, Winter said helpfully, "At least he isn't ashamed and hiding it. That would suck if he had intimacy with you and then pretended he didn't."

"See?" Dustin said, giving Winter a high five. "Really, I'm being a gentleman."

"Werewolves aren't gentlemen," Logan muttered. "No more high fives." His voice was way too snarly.

Beast yanked the passenger door open. "Finally." When he climbed up on the seat, he rocked the entire truck with his massive size.

Winter held onto the oh-shit-bar dramatically, and Emma thrashed around like she was caught in an earthquake. Logan and Dustin looked amused. Beast, however, did not. He poked the radio dial until blaring opera music blasted through the speakers, flipped them all off, then pulled his baseball cap over his face like he was going to sleep.

Emma loved him. She loved all of them. Beast with his mood-swings but protective nature, Logan with his quiet observations, dark past, and sweet demeanor with Winter. She loved that Winter was so bright and positive about everything. She could spin any bad day into a good one, and she was becoming a really good friend. And Dustin...well, she liked him best for a million reasons.

He was watching her with a wicked smile. *You want my dick*, he mouthed.

Stop it, she mouthed back.

I like your boobs.

Emma slowed her words and formed them carefully so he could catch them all. *Well, I like your hair and your tattoos.*

I like your eyes. The smile was dipping from his face, and he was getting more serious as Logan eased the truck onto the main road. *And your lips. I like those a lot. And this game because I get to watch those lips.*

I like that you didn't snore last night when you stayed over.

I liked that you snored like a freight train.

I did not!

How would you know? He tapped his ear and arched his eyebrow.

Oh, my gosh, do I really? That was news to her.

No.

He laughed when she shoved his arm.

Mean, she accused.

When Dustin pulled her hand to his lips in a flash, his smile disappeared completely. *But I'm trying to be better.*

"What are y'all doing?" Logan asked suspiciously.

Jerking his chin in Logan's direction, Dustin mouthed, *Psycho-baby*.

Emma giggled and shook her head. She wasn't going to get into a name war with the king of name-calling.

Winter stared at them with narrowed eyes. "I think you two are grosser than me and Logan."

"That's bullcrap," Dustin said. "My room is close to yours, *Winter Donovan*. You and Logan are loud. And super-gross. And you always have to be touching, and you always look at each other with those dumb googly eyes—"

"I'm never pairing up," Beast muttered from under his baseball cap. "You're all disgusting."

Emma frowned. Dustin said he'd been the head of a pride for a long time. He would have been paired up with lots of lionesses...right?

But when she looked up at Dustin to ask him, he looked just as confused as her and shrugged.

When Logan pulled onto the dirt road that led to the fledgling trailer park, Emma unbuckled and eased forward between the seats. She thought Beast would growl at her, but he gave her a grimace that was almost a smile instead. And when Emma rested her cheek on his muscular shoulder and made a happy sound, Beast didn't even shove her head away this time.

There was a brand new wooden sign over the entrance. *Blackwing Mobile Park* had been carved into it neatly, and in smaller letters just underneath, it read *Home of the D-Team*.

Emma laughed. It was perfect.

"Kane got the Novak Raven to make it," Logan said. "He's good at woodwork."

"Logan said wood," Dustin muttered as he pulled his cell from his back pocket.

"Is it just me, or is Kane starting to relax around us?" Winter asked.

"Well," Logan murmured, "he did sit on a dirty bathroom floor just to hang out with us, so I'd say yes. Except for Dustin. He still hates Dustin."

"Thanks, man," Dustin muttered, typing something into his phone.

"What are you doing?" Emma asked him.

"Inviting Kane and Rowan to the party for brownie points."

"Damn, you really do want to pledge to this crew," Logan said, pulling to a stop in front of his and Winter's doublewide. It was still getting electrical and plumbing hooked up, so they hadn't moved it yet, but soon. A wave of envy washed through Emma.

She didn't know if she and Dustin could pledge yet, and she was sick of living in the motel room. For a moment, she imagined her and Dustin coming up on their moving day. It wasn't fair to Winter, though, for her to be jealous, and Emma was really happy for her and Logan. They'd found a place, found home, and this, in this clearing, would be it for them. This would be safety and security. This would be their constant.

Suddenly, Beast snarled. As he swung toward her, Emma squeaked and threw herself against the backseat. He reached for Dustin. "What did you do to her?"

"What are you talking about?" Dustin said, ducking his swiping paw.

"Why the fuck does she smell sad?" he bellowed.

"Why aren't you buckled?" Winter yelled equally loudly.

"Everyone get out of my truck!" Logan also yelled.

Emma held onto Beast's arm, chanting, "He didn't do anything! He didn't do anything!" But now Beast was hanging halfway in the backseat with his hand around Dustin's throat. Dustin kicked him in the face, and though Beast's nose bled like a bloody fountain, he wouldn't loosen his grip. And now his eyes were bright gold. Fuck!

Panicked, Emma reached into her purse and pulled out her pepper spray, popped the top, and squirted a healthy dollop into Beast's face. The spray filled the cab of the truck like a fog, and the burn in Emma's eyes was instant. They all started screaming and yelling at once, scrabbling for doors, falling out of the truck, crawling on the ground.

"Fuck, Emma!" Logan yelled. "Why didn't you just knee him?"

"Don't yell at her!" Dustin said from where he was rolling on the ground rubbing his eyes.

Choking on the spray, Emma bolted for the blue cooler in the back, fumbled desperately to get it open, and pulled out bottled waters. She dumped one on her face and scrubbed her eyes as fast as she could. Her eyes were watering so bad she could barely see. She wanted to dump another one on her face immediately, but her guilt was real and deep, so she lobbed a bottle at each of the D-Team.

On accident, she pegged Beast in the face, and he roared a terrifying sound.

"No, no, no!" Winter screamed as a monstrous lion exploded from Beast.

He turned furious eyes directly at Dustin. Dear lord, he was as tall as the truck bed. Three times bigger than Winter's panther at least.

"Oh, my gosh," Emma choked out.

Dustin looked back at her. "Get out of here. Now, Emma!"

Beast stalked closer, his lips snarled back over impossibly long, white canines. Dustin Changed in an instant, and the snarling black wolf placed himself in front of Emma, backing her up slowly. She could barely see now, but something huge was coming in fast from the other side of the truck.

A monstrous grizzly tackled Beast, and then there was a panther in the fray, clawing, slapping, and hissing as the titan shifters went to war. Shit! She still had pepper spray, so she bolted for them. They were going to kill each other!

She emptied the entire damn canister, but all she got for her effort was a lion ass to her chest, which blasted her backward. She screeched as she hit the dirt, and now Dustin was in the fight, teeth sunk deep into Beast's back.

Her tailbone felt like it had just rocketed through her esophagus, but this was deadly bad, so she forced her way upward and to the back of the truck.

"Stop it, all of you!" she screamed as loud as she could as she lobbed water bottle after water bottle at them. A jug of Fireball Cinnamon Whisky hit Logan in the face, and he roared at her.

"What the fuck is going on?" Kane bellowed. "Change back! *Now!*" Power crackled through the air like lightning and, whoo, the dark dragon looked pissed.

Rowan was giggling behind him like this was

funny, but it most certainly wasn't. The D-Team had just done the most D-Team thing ever, and it was all Emma's fault.

The roaring turned to grunts of pain, and then there was a pile of naked people trying to untangle. Apparently somebody accidentally touched Winter's boob because Beast got popped in the jaw by Logan, and now the two were brawling in their human skins, just...blasting each other in the faces, fists connecting with sickening thuds. The sheer violence was terrifying.

Kane ripped Logan backward and shoved a hand on Beast's chest, then gave Dustin an I-fuckin'-dare-you glare when he trotted forward a couple steps.

"Fuck," Dustin said, then spat red into the grass. "For the record, this one isn't my fault."

"Separate! Logan, over there." Kane shoved him toward one side of the truck. "Beast, over there." He shoved the tatted-up lion shifter to the other. "Dustin, stay right there, and Winter, I swear to God, if you don't stop stalking Beast, I'm going to burn your tail hair off."

Winter froze all hunched over, her eyes still glowing gold. Everyone was super naked but Emma, who gave Kane a two-fingered wave when he glared at her.

"What is wrong with you?" Kane asked to no one in particular.

"Beast is a psychopath, and so is Logan," Dustin muttered unhelpfully. "I have a submissive problem, Emma's perfect, and Winter uses her claws too damn much when she fights her *own fucking people*." He glared at Winter and pressed a hand to a deep set of bleeding claw marks across his chest.

"That was a rhetorical question!" Kane barked out.

"I use just the right amount of claws when you three are being territorial assholes," Winter smarted off.

"Well, I hope you get scabies," Dustin said. "Emma, woman, can you come stand behind me. I feel all crazy right now, and you're too far away for me to protect. My eyes burn like I've stuck hot pokers in them, and thanks again *Kane* for the forced Change."

"Are you done?" Kane bellowed.

"My dick hurts," Dustin muttered, cupping himself. "I think someone kicked it in the fight."

Kane arched one black eyebrow and looked

terrifying.

"Now I'm done," Dustin murmured, averting his gaze.

Emma pursed her lips because Rowan stood right behind Kane, biting her bottom lip like she was holding back her laughter. Her eyes were doing the laughing for her. The Second of the Blackwing Crew let off a soft peel of giggles.

"It's not funny," Kane said in an exasperated tone.

"I mean…it's kind of funny," Rowan said. "Look at them. They all look like they're crying, their faces are all red, it smells like Mace, and you just know the story behind this is *so* dumb."

"It was all my fault," Emma said, womaning up. "Beast was choking Dustin, and he's mine to protect, but I don't have, you know, claws or teeth, so I meant to only pepper spray Beast, but I got all of us, and then I hit Beast in the face with a water bottle, and he turned into this…this…monster-lion. I mean…" Emma spread her arms as far as she could. "He was huge. And then Logan and Winter and Dustin all changed, and my eyes really burn, really bad, but it's all my fault. All of it, but I might be going blind." She blinked rapidly, tears of pain streaking down her cheeks.

But now Kane was fighting a smile. With a sigh, he hooked his hands on his hips and muttered, "You're all a bunch of idiots." But the sting was gone from his voice. He bent down and picked up a water, then handed it to Winter. "Rowan and I will fire up the grill. Get yourselves together, Crew." And then shaking his head, Kane led Rowan toward the back of Logan and Winter's trailer. Emma could've sworn Dark Kane muttered, "I need a drink," as he passed, but he was speaking too softly so she could've been mistaken.

Emma turned back around to the others, who were now pouring water over their faces and scrubbing their eyes. "Are you mad at me?"

"Yes," Logan and Beast said simultaneously.

Winter shook her head. "I'm not."

"Hell no." Dustin shook his wet hair like a dog. "The real shit-starter in all of this was Beast."

"Me?" Beast growled.

"Yeah, none of this would've happened if you'd kept your hands to yourself and stopped trying to kill everyone all the time! Emma was protecting me. You started it."

Beast lunged, but Dustin didn't back down. Huh. Usually Dustin exposed his neck pretty quick after he got hurt, but he seemed in no mood to deal with Beast's beastly mood. Logan could barely keep them separated since his hands kept slipping on their wet chests. Swinging dicks were everywhere. Emma was trying not to look, really she was, but it was like three super-models having a wet and naked party. Winter was staring, too, with her mouth hanging open.

"We should go," Emma murmured as the boys started yelling at each other.

"So many abs," Winter said.

"So many," Emma agreed.

"My eyes still really burn." Winter turned toward her, and Emma giggled sympathetically. Winter's wet, dark hair was plastered to the sides of her face, and her eyes were red and swollen.

"Does my make-up still look okay?" Emma joked.

Winter blasted a laugh and shook her head. "Not at all."

"Do you think I'll still get laid tonight?" she teased.

"Yes!" Dustin called. "Yes, you will. Stop!" He wrenched his hand out of Beast's grip and jogged over to her. He tilted her head back gently and winced at whatever it was he saw there. "Shortcake, never use pepper spray as a weapon again. Please."

"Don't worry. I learned my lesson. I think I bruised my butt when I fell."

"Nooo, not your butt," Dustin teased gently. "It was perfect, and it takes you humans years to heal."

The redness and swelling on his face was already fading away, and the claw marks had already stopped bleeding. "Not fair," she complained, frowning.

"Yeah, werewolf healing is some of the best in the game. We're the fastest to recover. He threw a middle finger to the others who were still washing their faces. "Suck it, suckers."

Emma pouted. She wanted healing powers. Her eyes felt like she'd just come out of a smoke-filled burning building. She was going to be the only one who looked like death warmed over tonight after the others had healed up.

Dustin pulled a plastic bin from the back of the truck to rest on the open tailgate, then popped the lid and dug through until he found a pair of jeans.

"You brought extra clothes?"

"We all did," Dustin explained. "This fight isn't a

big shocker. Kane is building a crew of unstable nut-jobs."

He gathered his shoes off the ground where they lay in a mess of tattered clothes. He flipped his damp hair to the side and dressed while she pulled out the biggest bin of supplies she could carry with her shrimpy human arms. Dustin stacked a bin on the cooler and carried them easily, his gait smooth like they weighed nothing. She, on the other hand, was trying to look tough as her arms were nearly pulled from their sockets.

Dustin had a really nice back, especially all flexed like this. Powerful legs were tucked into those sexy jeans, and his hair was mussed as though he'd just gotten out of the shower. When he turned around and walked backward in front of her, she thought he would joke with her, but his face was serious. His sandy-blond brows lowered thoughtfully. "Hey, Emma?"

"Yeah?"

He eased to a stop at the side of the trailer, then set down his supplies and took hers from her arms, too. He approached slowly and pulled her against his warm chest. The weather was chilly, but he felt like a furnace. "You aren't a shifter, so you don't realize how dangerous that was back there. You don't feel how bad off Logan's animal is, or Beasts, or mine. You're safe with Winter, but that's it." He eased back and let her see his lips as he lowered his voice. "It was reckless to charge a group of warring animals like that. Next time it could be worse than a bruised butt. If I ever ask you to run, I need to know you'll trust me and do it. Not because I'm trying to boss you around. I know you're a strong woman who knows her mind, but because I need to know that when it comes down to it, you can help me keep you safe. Swear it."

She waited for the punchline. Dustin was rarely serious like this, but his frown stayed in place, and he was leveling her with such an intense look, she had no choice but to give him the promise he wanted. "I swear I'll listen. I forget sometimes that...you know."

"No, tell me."

"That I'm not one of you."

She wanted him to tell her she was wrong. She wanted him to say, 'No, Emma, you are just like us. You are Crew.' But he didn't.

Instead, he shook his head slowly and sighed. "You have to stay out of the animal fights. You don't heal like us. One swipe from a paw, and you could bleed out before I can stop it. Or one accidental bite, and you're Turned. Especially around Logan and Beast, Emma, *especially* them. They don't have any control."

He was pleading with her for understanding with such sincerity, she nodded and whispered, "Okay."

Dustin stared down at her a moment longer, then kissed her lips. When he disengaged with a sweet smacking sound, he picked up both bins and the cooler, gave her one last worried glance over his shoulder, and then disappeared around the corner of the house.

For the first time in her life, Emma felt weak. She'd been raised with vampires in a strong and loyal coven. Her family had never made her feel different, even if she was human and hearing impaired. Sure, they could've drank her dry at any moment, but Emma had never felt at risk.

But here with the Blackwings, where fire-breathing dragons ruled the mountains and the titans of the crew lusted for blood and brawls, she was at the bottom of the food chain.

And her weakness wasn't only a risk for her anymore.

It put the man she loved at risk, too.

TWELVE

He'd hurt Emma.

Dustin flipped the steaks on the grill, took a swig of his beer, then cast her another sideways glance. Instinct wouldn't let him take his eyes off her for long. Not when she smelled sad.

She was sitting in a purple bag chair between Winter and Rowan. The other two females were chattering happily over her, but his mate was staring off into the nothing. He missed her smile. That's what he wanted to give her, not frowns and sad eyes.

He wouldn't admit it, but he'd bought black bag chairs for all the other Blackwings but purple for her because it was the color she wore the most. He hoped it was her favorite color. The hair rose on the back of his neck, and when he looked over at Kane, the alpha was sitting in a chair, hand resting on his mate's leg as he stared thoughtfully at Dustin. His wolf didn't want to give the dragon his back, but Dustin forced his gaze away and paid attention to the steaks. There was no doubt in his mind the dark dragon knew exactly who Dustin was. He knew *what* he was—a traitor. It was beyond Dustin why Kane hadn't killed him yet. It made no sense that he wasn't a pile of ash right now sitting in the belly of the dragon.

God, she'd gone straight for Beast with that damn pepper spray. Dustin had been fine, wasn't even close to being choked out, but his girl had gone protective immediately. She would make an amazing she-wolf. She had those instincts to jump in a fight and wreak havoc. Little hellion. He bet her wolf would be gorgeous. If he Turned her, would she be a black wolf like him? Would she be submissive like him? Would she be broken like him? Or would she be stronger? Didn't matter. He would never bite her. She didn't want that from him, and now a big part of him thought she was making the right choice. Werewolves were fucked up on a good day. Vampires, too, but they weren't as unstable. She had a good head on her shoulders. Emma would make one hell of a vampire. And that was a good thing, because soon, he wouldn't be around to protect her anymore. Either Kane or Axton was going to off him. He just didn't know which one yet.

"Dude, cut it out," Logan snarled from right beside him.

Dustin startled and swallowed down the growl that was rattling his throat. He hadn't realized he was doing it. The steaks were medium rare and cooked enough, so Dustin shoved Logan to give himself some room and pulled all the steaks but one onto a plate. Emma was human. She wouldn't like her meat bloody.

The bear shifter flashed him a frown as he made to take the plate to the table Winter had bought for the back porch. But before he left, Logan sighed an irritated sound, turned back around, and lowered his voice. "Are you okay, man?"

Dustin wanted to pop off, but he was so shocked the ex-mercenary cared, he couldn't think of a single witty response. Instead he answered, "I'll hold. Just working through some stuff." Like betraying his damn pack. And not only his pack but his flesh-and-blood brother. Everything had gotten so messed up.

Looking uncomfortable, Logan shifted his gaze to the exposed beams of the porch ceiling. He cleared his throat once, twice. "If you ever need to talk, you can say words to me, and I will try not to kill you."

It was the nicest thing Logan had ever said to him, but this bro-shit was strange, so Dustin grunted and nodded, and thankfully Logan understood because he spun and stomped off with the food. Holy shit, that was weird. Kind of cool, but weird.

Winter was looking at him all mushy, so Dustin flipped her off and then yanked the piles of asparagus off the foil and onto a giant plate with a pair of tongs.

Emma slipped her arms around his waist from behind and rested her cheek on his spine. "I'm sorry," she murmured.

Dustin slid his hand over hers just to keep her in place. "Crazy girl, there is nothing to apologize for."

She sighed. "I texted my mom. I told her it's time to talk about the Turn. I don't want to be the cause for anyone getting hurt. Not the crew, and especially not you."

Dustin's heart banged against his chest hard and fast. Now? Sure, he'd accepted she was going vamp, but this soon? He didn't feel ready.

She tightened her grip on his waist, and he forced himself to move. He inhaled a steadying breath and took her steak off the grill. "What will happen when she Turns you?"

"She'll drain me, I'll die, and she'll keep my body safe until I rise a few days later."

Dustin swallowed bile. Sure, Emma would come back a supe, but to do so, she had to die first. He turned off the grill and spun slowly in her arms so she could read his lips when he murmured, "Does Kane know?"

"Yes. I was open with it in my first interview. He knows of my coven. They are some of the good ones. Quiet pillars in their community. They are helpers, not hurters."

"How do they eat?" He couldn't help the bitterness in his voice.

"They pay feeders. It's all voluntary. It's part of the reason I've been saving up. I want to afford to pay feeders so I don't ever go into a feeding frenzy. I don't want to hurt people."

Dustin thought of her lips on someone else's neck and gritted his teeth against the urge to bite her here and now and stop that from ever happening.

Selfish creature. This is what she wants.

With a sigh, Dustin brushed her hair behind her shoulders and told her, "I'll be your feeder." He leaned down, kissed her neck once, held her stunned gaze for a moment more, and then took the rest of the food to the table.

Kane was still watching him, but his eyes didn't look quite as full of hatred right now.

"What?" Dustin gritted out. He was really fucking tired of everyone watching him like he was a time bomb. Granted, he *was* a time bomb, but still. Between Kane eavesdropping and Beast stalking him for funsies, this was all getting a little annoying.

"I thought I had you figured out, wolf," Kane said, angling his head and relaxing back in his chair. "Now I'm not so sure."

"Well, there was your first problem, *Alpha*." Dustin offered him an empty smile. "No use trying to figure out a werewolf."

"Hmm," Kane rumbled noncommittally. His eyes were glowing that iridescent green with the long dragon pupils, but he wasn't sneering. In fact, the End of Days was smiling ever so slightly at Dustin. A first.

And creepy.

He was probably planning what seasoning to eat him with.

****

Gray Dog was a beggar. Emma loved him, especially after Rowan had given him a bath and made him smell like honeysuckle. He wore a black leather collar with silver spikes and a pink bow on a tuft of hair right on the top of his head, a testament to Roe and Kane's disagreements behind the scenes on how to raise their fur baby. Gray Dog didn't seem to mind, though, and didn't even try to scratch the bow out. He was a mutt, but Emma would bet her britches he had a lot of Irish Wolfhound in him. Wiry, coarse gray fur, long, lanky legs, barrel chest but lean, and with a great smile. It was one of those doggy grins where his tongue always hung out to the side while he stared with his big brown eyes. Like he was doing now as he whined for Emma to sneak him a bite of her leftover steak.

Dustin didn't hesitate, just flipped the dog a piece of his without a thought. Kane growled. Dustin shrugged. Rowan giggled. And Emma fell a little harder for the werewolf sitting beside her.

"So, tell me, *Dustin*," Kane said around a bite of fruit salad. "What did you do with my dog all that time you had him?"

Dustin tossed his now empty plate on the table and leaned back in his chair, pulled Emma's feet into his lap, and leveled Kane with a look. "We watched TV every night, he ate table scraps and dog food, and I took him to the dog park three times a week until he banged this poodle and we got banned on account of you not neutering him, so now he probably has some ugly puppies somewhere." Dustin gave another hollow smile. "Congrats, grandpa."

Something was up with him and Kane. The tension had always been there, but lately it was thick as fog.

"I don't know. We just did regular shit," Dustin ended, linking his hands behind his head.

"But you let me think this entire time that my dog was murdered."

"Yeah, well, he wasn't. He was having a vacation. I even gave him a flea bath. Mostly because he gave my wolf fleas, and it sucked. His bow looks extra stupid, by the way."

"Heeey," Rowan drawled with a disapproving

grimace. She leaned forward and covered Gray Dog's ears. "He's sensitive."

"False, I called him Smelly Motherfucker the entire time he lived with me. He never got his feelings hurt, and he answers to it now. Come here, Smelly Motherfucker."

Gray Dog gave Dustin a canine grin and scrabbled over to him. The dog licked under his chin while Dustin baby-talked him. God, Emma had never considered loving animals a sexy quality in a man, but it really was. Gray Dog was getting so worked up and happy his wagging tail was a blur, and he was whining between licks.

Dustin ripped the bow out of his hair and tossed it in Rowan's lap. "Who's a handsome tough guy now?" he asked, scratching under his spiked collar. Dustin sniffed him and grimaced. "Why does he smell like douche water?"

Logan was standing on a ladder wrapping the new porch beams in outdoor lights. "I don't even want to ask how you know what douche water smells like."

Emma and Winter snickered, Rowan twirled the bow in her hands and grinned proudly, Kane shook his head in annoyance, and Beast downed an entire beer in one long swig and looked like he hated everything. And all was right in her crew.

Her crew. She could really have this. Sure, there were conditions, but they didn't seem so bad anymore. A bite-mark on Dustin, and they could both be in. They could both be home. She was turning vamp soon anyways, and he'd already told her he wanted to be her feeder. She would be biting him then whenever she needed sustenance so what was a bite-mark in the grand scheme of things? Now they felt like a shoo-in to register for the Blackwings.

"Kane?" Emma asked.

"Yep?"

"Which concrete pad is for me and Dustin?"

"The one right next to this one. I figured you would want to be close to Winter. Beast will be on the end, in the back of the trailer park where he asked to be."

"It's closest to the woods," Beast said gruffly.

"We're going to be one big, happy family," Winter said.

"I meant to say it's farthest away from all of you," Beast corrected. He gave a wicked smile and a nod like he'd won some contest.

"Do you want me to make you a trophy for biggest asshole in the crew?" Dustin asked, twisting a few napkins together.

"Yeah. I'd love that. I'll put it right in my front window as a warning for you fuckers to stay off my lawn."

Dustin handed him what looked suspiciously like a penis he'd fashioned from the napkins. "Congratulations, Beast. We're all so proud of you and support you in your endeavors."

Beast yanked it out of his hand and growled a terrifying noise.

"What happened to your face?" Emma asked.

"Not polite," Beast said, eyes on the woods.

"Why not? People ask me all the time about my hearing aids. I don't get my panties in a twist."

Beast cast her an angry glare, then gave his attention back to the woods, offering them all a perfect view of the deep claw marks that marred half of his face. "I fell," he said sarcastically.

Emma tapped her hearing aid and murmured, "Me, too." She wouldn't get anywhere with Beast. He was an enigma set behind sky-high walls a mile thick.

And really, right now, she wanted to go see the place that might be home someday. "Come on," she said, tugging Dustin up out of his chair. "Let's go see our house."

"Wait, is this the bat signal?"

"No, you horny werewolf, I actually just want to see where our future house will be."

"Living with Dustin won't be as fun as you think," Logan muttered from up on the ladder.

"Oh, and living with you is going to be a cake-walk? Please," Dustin muttered as Emma dragged him down the porch stairs. "You're lucky Winter's type is 'lunatic.'"

When Dustin scooped her up in his arms suddenly, Emma squealed and clutched onto his neck. "What are you doing?"

"Walking you across the threshold."

"Aaaaw!" Her cheeks heated with pleasure, and she hugged him tighter as he did indeed walk over where the door would be.

The concrete was freshly poured but dry to walk on. "Kitchen," she said, pointing. It would be the same layout as Winter and Logan's home, and she'd been in there several times just to memorize the layout and fantasize about her own house.

"Living room," he said, jerking his chin to the right.

"Bedroom—"

"My favorite room," Dustin said with a naughty glint to his eyes.

Emma giggled as he lowered her to her feet directly in the middle of the concrete. His eyes went serious in a second. "Are you sure, Emma? With me? It's…"

"It's what?"

"I don't know, a risk. And it's still not a done deal. I have to work out some major shit still to swing this. It's scary to imagine things that might not come true."

"Are you backing out?"

"No, no." He shook his head hard. "Not me. But if something happens to me…"

She hated the sound of that. "Like what?"

"Or, you know, you might back out when you figure out who I really am."

Emma smiled up at him. "Silly wolf, don't you know?"

Dustin cocked his head. "Know what?"

Sliding her hands up his shoulders, she

murmured, "I see you. The real you. Maybe the crew doesn't yet, but I do. You didn't hide well enough from me."

Dustin searched her face with an unfathomable expression. His eyes glowed with such beautiful intensity, it threatened to take her breath away. He signed clumsily, *If I could have my way, I would give this all to you.*

You will, she signed back slowly in the simple alphabet so he could understand her.

His chest rose with his deep inhalation, and he pulled her into a hug, stood their swaying them gently from side to side in the middle of their pretend house as they watched the sun setting over the mountains. Dusk was putting on quite the show tonight. The sky was painted in soft yellows and pinks, and thin clouds dotted the horizon. The two towering mountains behind the trailer park created a perfect valley between them to watch the sun sink to the horizon.

Dustin sat on the concrete, right in the middle of what would hopefully someday be their living room, and pulled her down between his legs. It wasn't often Dustin got quiet, and she would have worried except he was still touching her. He was still showing her affection, and the glowing in his eyes had faded with each passing minute.

Emma relaxed her shoulder blades against his chest as he wrapped his arms around her and settled his cheek against hers. "I got you something," he said against her ear.

"A present?"

One nod. "I had all these plans for when I said 'I love you' for the first time, but earlier, it just felt like the right time."

"It was," she said. "It was perfect. I'll never forget it."

Dustin was quiet for a minute before he said, "Do you know what werewolves say about home?"

Emma shook her head.

"Home is where you rest your bones. It's not a specific place, or person, or even somewhere permanent. Wolves roam. Packs roam. Settling territories is hard because no one wants us near their towns. And rightly so. We tend to ruin things. When I was growing up, we moved every year from rental home to rental home. I hated that the pack was always on the move, and my parents had to take us wherever the alpha decided. It's not like with crews, you understand? There's no working together unless we are hunting. There is the alpha's law, and you just hope to get into a pack with a good alpha who will keep you alive longer. Pack is for survival, not for a happy life. There aren't a lot of mated pairs for werewolves. What woman is going to put up with our shit? Most of the girls in the pack I grew up in were turned against their will and had nowhere else to go. They were always scared. Skittish. It's how I thought women were supposed to be. My mom was one of them. Weak around my dad, strong for me and my brother. She understood the need for her sons to be dominant in the pack so we could be safe, and when I came along..." Dustin swallowed hard. "She wasn't disappointed in me. She was disappointed that my life would be stunted. She could see my future. So could my dad, so could my brother, so could I. So she made sure I had the best shot possible to survive into adulthood. She pushed me in school where she didn't with my dominant brother. It was hard because we were moving around so much, but she devoted herself to making sure I got the best education. Good schools, college—she was relentless. At the time, I didn't understand why until Axton chose me for the pack he was building. Me, a submissive, and Axton was one of the most dominant wolves in the world at the time."

"Why did he pick you?"

"Because I built a business that could support his pack."

Emma turned her back on the sunset and settled between his legs facing him. "You funded your pack?"

Dustin nodded. "That's what has kept me alive this long. I built teams of marketers, elite teams, and sold their services to huge corporations. That's how I started out. It was beneficial to the teams because I could negotiate more money for them, and beneficial for me because I made huge commissions on each team I successfully sold to these companies. So if one of the pack lost a job, or had a hard time paying bills, or fuck, just didn't want to work, I took care of them."

Whoa, this was unexpected. Dustin was thoroughly educated and a clever businessman. All of his perverted jokes and lack of seriousness had thrown her way off track. "That's how you afford your car."

He huffed a laugh and rested his elbows on her

bent knees, linked his hands behind her back. "That's the one splurge I ever did for just me. Axton was pissed that I wasted pack money, but I didn't care on this one. I earned all that money and fed it into the pack as an investment on my survival, but I wanted a fast car. I wanted somewhere I could just cruise when shit got too heavy. I wanted a place to sleep when we were moving around and fighting like fucking...well...werewolves."

"Axton moved you around a lot?"

"Yeah, his reputation preceded him wherever we went to claim territory. He is a bulldozer and a killer. He's killed a dozen of our own kind just to get to where he is, but that's what alphas do."

"Kane didn't do that."

"Kane's not a werewolf. The culture is different, Emma. We're separate from other shifters."

Emma ran her knuckles along the short scruff on his jawline and rested her cheek against his arm. "Home is where you rest your bones. Sounds like a sad life to never understand what a real home is."

Dustin stared off into the woods and shook his head. "I never knew what I was missing, and I never cared until I met you. Until I came here and saw how

187

a crew could work. How it could be under Kane."

"You want that now?"

He dipped his chin once. "When I was a kid, my mom, she planted flowers everywhere at every rental house we moved into. We would stay there a year tops, so she would never get to see her gardens in full bloom, and it was kind of tragic, you know? She was so sad with my dad, but she was all smiles when we would work in her gardens. I think she was bright before my dad put a wolf in her. One of those naturally happy people, like you and Winter and Rowan. So, growing up, each house we would move to, I would make a wish for my mom. Every time the clock turned to the number 11:11 or 10:10, I would put my finger on the numbers, close my eyes, and wish we could stay in a house long enough for my mom to see her garden in bloom."

Emma's eyes prickled with tears at the imaginings of Dustin as a sweet child, making wishes for his momma. "Did it ever work?"

Dustin's lips pursed into a thin line, the expression at odds with his naturally smiling face. He shook his head. "Not in time. She stopped gardening when I was in college. She just...quit. Stopped smiling, stopped laughing. And anyway, my parents' pack is still on the move. It's the way the alpha likes to operate, so they do what he says. I asked her once what her favorite flower was. I remember we were in this rental house up in Portland, and it rained a lot while we were there, but that day, it was sunny. I was weeding. God, I was always weeding with her because it was mindless work and she was nice to me. She didn't shame me for being submissive, so I was squatted down in the dirt, maybe ten years old, and I asked her, 'Mom, what's your favorite flower?' She was standing beside me, the sun behind her like a halo, making her look beautiful, like an angel, and she smiled so big. It had been a bad week with Dad, and I'd missed her smile. She pointed to this green vine with these little purple flowers that looked like trumpets. Morning Glories, she called them. She said they were her favorite because they only opened up during the day when the sun was out. At night, the flowers closed up so they could keep the darkness away."

Dustin reached into his back pocket and handed her a packet of Morning Glory seeds. "Last night I wished on 10:10 and 11:11 that I could plant you a garden here, and that I would live long enough to watch it bloom with you." When his eyes filled with deep emotion, he blinked hard, then stood. "I'm going to grab a beer. Do you want anything?" His voice cracked on the last word.

Emma didn't understand what was happening. "Dustin, you *will* live long enough, you silly wolf. Your wish will come true."

"You don't understand," he gritted out. He angled his face away from her, and his teeth were clenched now. "Those wishes never come true." He dipped his blazing gaze to the packet of seeds in her hand, then turned and strode for the trailer without looking back.

And now Emma was left with this hollow feeling, as if he'd given her all of his secrets and none of them, all at once.

THIRTEEN

Pocket buzzing incessantly, Dustin's phone went off again. Only the Valdoro pack and the Blackwing Crew had this number, and he'd just spent all evening with the Blackwings, so it wasn't them calling. He couldn't put this off any longer.

He'd avoided Axton and Jace's calls like the plague over the last few days, ever since they'd seen him and Emma in the woods. Ever since they'd called him, howling, drawing his wolf back. If Emma hadn't been there distracting him, Axton would've succeeded. He would've dragged Dustin right back to him, and hurt Emma. Jace would have hurt her too, if Axton commanded it. They didn't care about hurting women. They didn't care about anything.

And once upon a time, Dustin had convinced himself he was the same as them. As if he was exactly like all the other psychotic werewolves in the world—normal for a wolf, even if he'd always been on the fringe. But over the past couple of weeks, such a strong desire to protect not only Emma, but the other Blackwings, had presented inside of him. He really was a broken wolf.

Somewhere in their history, wolves had separated themselves from other shifters and began culling their submissives. And without people to protect, their wolves had gone mad with bloodlust that, honestly, werewolves didn't put much effort into controlling.

And Axton was the most dangerous of all.

Oh, Dustin had grown up with him. He'd watched him mature from a rambunctious pup to a heartless alpha who functioned best with blood on his hands.

It wasn't as if Dustin had been ignoring the danger. On the contrary, he'd been watching Emma like a hawk. Stalking her like Beast had stalked him, but not for the same reasons. He was on a mission to keep her safe no matter the cost. Because if Emma didn't exist in this world, it was nothing but a dark and empty place. Like Axton's soul.

Dustin was going to die tonight.

He ran his hands through his hair and rested his elbows on his knees. He was sitting on the foot of his bed in the motel room. He'd been given one job by his pack, one that could've saved his brother— vengeance. And he couldn't do it. Not anymore. Somewhere along the way, he'd grown this bond with the Blackwings and sewn his soul to Emma. Axton had called him a grenade. His brother had told him he would destroy the Blackwings, and therefore the Bloodrunners, from the inside out. Axton said he would tell him when to pull the pin, but now it was his pack who would lose out.

Dustin was nobody's grenade.

He would die before he hurt the people he'd grown to care about in Kane's Mountains. He'd die a thousand deaths before he hurt Emma.

She was confused. He'd put on the show for the rest of the night after he'd given her the Morning Glory seeds. He'd joked and annoyed the shit out of the Blackwings. God, he wanted a few more days with her, and with his new friends. Friends? Werewolves didn't have fucking friends. They had pack. This crew shit had messed with his head so thoroughly he didn't understand where he belonged anymore. Where he fit. Maybe he fit nowhere. Perhaps he'd always fit nowhere.

You fit with her.

His wolf was a wise one. He'd always had a level head for a monster. Dustin wanted to scream and trash the hotel room. He wanted to rip up the mattress, claw at the walls, overturn the furniture, ruin this room as his last act. But a flash of Emma's journal flickered through his mind. It was the picture of him striding for her, desperation to hold her written all over his face. *I know you're still good.*

His last few hours should be a gift for Emma. She didn't realize it yet, but she would. Emma deserved so much better than him. What was the point of feeding the anger and trashing the room as his last defiant act? It wasn't fair he'd met her so close to the end or he'd gotten a glimpse of a happy life with the Blackwing Crew before he got his throat ripped out for real this time. But then again, life wasn't fair.

He was going to miss everything. Emma turning vamp, her coming into her own power, the Blackwings solidifying into one badass, albeit fucked-up, crew. He would miss holding Emma every night and being there when she cried. He would miss hearing her sing. He would miss her big green eyes looking up at him like he was worth a damn. Her little heart-shaped birthmark on the inside of her elbow, the way she shifted her weight when she was flattered by something he'd said, how cute her ears were, even when she had the aids in. Her blushes, tits, wit, strength, curves, happy smiles, sad smiles, hair blowing in her face when the breeze hit her just right, her in firefly woods, her graceful hands as she signed to cuss him out or tell him she loved him.

He was going to miss her love.

Fuck. Dustin swallowed the howl of agony that clawed up the back of his throat and forced himself to stand. He pulled the phone from his back pocket as it vibrated again. "What?" he snarled out.

"Pack meeting, asshole," Jace said. "Bring the girl."

There was snarling in the background, the crazy kind.

"I don't have a girl."

"Fucking lie! If your voice didn't give you away, the fact you haven't answered our damn calls for three days does. And if both of those failed, we saw you fuck her, Dustin. Except it wasn't fucking, was it? You were bonding to her. You were making love, like the stupid fuck you are."

The snarling got louder. Axton was bad off. Jace was lucky to still be breathing. Axton was the grenade, and his pin had been pulled the day the Bloodrunner Dragon had destroyed the pack. Dustin used to hate Harper Keller for what she'd done, but now he could see it clearly. She'd defended that girl, Lexi. She'd avenged Axton and the pack's attempted murder on her. Dustin would've done the same thing if the pack hunted Emma, and he wasn't even her damn alpha. He'd wanted to save his brother, but now he could see Axton had brought all of these consequences on himself. He was the one who had gotten his pack burned and eaten by the Bloodrunner Dragon. It wasn't Harper's fault. It was Axton's.

"Dustin! I swear to God if you don't answer me now, we are coming to that shitty motel and dragging your bitch out by her hair. Fucking meet us. Two hours. Same spot we always meet. Just you and the girl, do you understand me?"

Dustin stared at a framed watercolor of a man in

a boat fishing all alone on a pond. "Two hours, I'll be there." He ended the call.

There was no way in hell he would bring Emma to Axton. She was human and fragile, his to protect. He didn't want her anywhere near when he went to battle to earn his freedom from the Valdoro pack. He wanted her to live. No, he *needed* it. She had to exist. He could go to hell easier if he took the rest of the pack with him into the flames. If he died for a reason—protecting Emma, the Blackwings, and the Bloodrunners—he could stomach leaving that sliver of happiness that had settled into his life over the last weeks.

Two hours.

Two hours to say goodbye.

When the alarm dinged on his phone, he looked down. *10:10.* Time to make a wish, and he better make this one count.

I wish Emma happiness when I'm gone.

FOURTEEN

Emma dumped her pile of laundry onto the bed and began sorting through it in search of T-shirts. She was weird and liked to fold one category of clothes at a time. John at the front desk had been nice enough to give her the keys to the laundry room, even though it was supposed to close at eight. When she got into the trailer, she was going to make John a big batch of brownies for always being so nice to her and the other D-Teamers.

Outside, Beast, Logan, and Winter were sitting on the curb talking about something way too low for her to hear. But she could hear Winter's laughter every once in a while, which always brought a smile to Emma's face. Right after folding her clothes, she was going to go out and join them and hope Dustin was over whatever had been bothering him earlier. She missed him. Sure, she'd just spent the evening with him, but he'd worn his fake smile too much. Something was going on in that head of his, something he didn't want her to see, and she hated it.

Any distance between them now hurt in really surprising ways.

Her eyes flashed to the pack of flower seeds on the nightstand. Had he realized he'd bought her flowers she would never see bloom? As soon as she turned vamp, the only thing she could hope to see was the closed flower buds at night, in the darkness, where she would dwell. A part of her wished she could be a shifter instead. Stupid ears and stupid hearing impairment. Without it, the choice would've been easy. Her whole life she'd prepared to be a vampire, but now she wanted to be like Dustin. She wanted his bite, wanted to run the woods with him, wanted to fit into the crew better, wanted to be Dustin's tiny pack within the Blackwings.

She wanted to be like him so neither of them would ever feel different or alone again.

A knock sounded on the door, but before she

could tell them to, "Hang on, I'm coming," the door lock clicked and Dustin sauntered in, pocketing the key card. He looked like sex on a stick in a tight black sweater, dark jeans, and his hair flipped to the side. He'd probably done that out of habit, but it looked mussed and sexy as hell. His blue and green eyes collided with hers, and a smile stretched his face. It was slight, but a real one this time. Relief.

She squeaked and ran to him, jumped up in his arms, and wrapped her legs around him. "I like you having a key."

He chuckled too low for her to hear, but she could feel the vibration against her cheek. Easing back and giving her a view of his lips, he asked, "You want some help?"

"With folding laundry?"

"Any chance for me to touch your panties, I'll take it. Even chores."

She laughed and rubbed her nose against his. God, that was so dorky, but his smile got a little bigger.

"John gave me a bag of popcorn when I was doing laundry earlier. I can pop it and we can put on a movie. You can rent them for two dollars. It can be like a room date."

"Sounds perfect." His tone sounded different, a little off, a little sad, and his eyes weren't dancing like they usually did.

"Are you okay?"

"Yeah." He kissed her gently, then brushed his tongue past her lips on the second sip of her mouth. Easing back way too soon, he said, "I'm just having a weird night. A room date is just what I need to set me right again."

Emma grinned. "Good. Glad I can help. And I hope you are good at folding because I have very specific tastes in folded clothes."

"High maintenance." He grabbed a pair of mismatched socks and wadded them together. "How's that."

"I knew you would be bad at this."

"What? How?" He folded a pair of her see-through lacy panties in half.

"Because you're bad at everything, naturally."

Dustin snorted and held up a finger. "One, I'm good at sex."

"Okay, I'll give you that. You're great at humping."

"Thank you." He held up a second finger. "Two, I'm a decent driver."

"Slow driver," she mumbled.

"To keep you safe, human, and three, I'm pretty good at pissing everyone off. Beast just tried to trip me when I passed him outside."

"Why?"

"Because I told him it was me who broke into his room and ate all of his pizza bagel bites. And popsicles. And I kept hiding his shampoo and shaving cream in different spots in his room every day. I drank the whole bottle of moonshine he kept hidden in the air vent, but I replaced it with the empty mason jar. I was also pissing in his toilet three times a day without flushing just to make him think he'd gone crazy."

Emma laughed and shook her head as she worked on another T-shirt. "That's my man. Beast is a little scary, though. Why did you admit to all that?"

Dustin's smile dipped from his lips. "I felt like confessing my sins tonight. I bought him a new jar of moonshine, but he's still mad. Thank God. A smiling Beast would be weird."

"So weird. What sins do you have to confess to

me?"

Dustin cast her a quick glance, then gave his attention back to the pair of comfy cottons he was folding. "Sometimes I sneak in your room when you are sleeping just to watch you."

Oh, this was serious. And also unsettling because she hadn't known that part at all. "Why do you do that?"

"Because I like the way your face looks when you sleep. Like you don't have a care in the world. Your lips go all pouty, and your hair sits wild on the pillow. And you smell different in your sleep. You smell so good when you are awake, but your sleep smell is like a secret that only I know." He smiled brightly. "Plus, I like the way you snore."

She shoved him and laughed.

"Tell me something good," he said suddenly, his eyes downcast and his hair hiding his face.

"Something real or something make-believe?"

"One of each."

"Okay, something real. I remember when I was brought home from Russia. My parents had traveled to pick me up from the orphanage and fill out all the paperwork. I was scared of them because they had pale skin, and their eyes changed colors. Even though they tried to hide it, they were hungry on their trip and couldn't help their fangs being out. I was only six and didn't understand about vampires except the scary stories people told me. But on the plane ride home, my ears were popping because of the altitude, and they hurt. I'd never flown before, and I was crying softly because I didn't want to be weak around the vampires. But my mom scooped me up in her lap and hugged me. I fought it for a few minutes, but I was really crying about everything, not just my ears hurting, you know? Leaving Russia, leaving the orphanage I'd lived in my whole life, not really understanding where I was going, or why vampires wanted me as their kid. And I remember my mom crying, face all buried against my neck, like she knew it was more than the pain, and she whispered, 'You're safe. We're going to take care of you for always.' And I remember clutching onto her blouse. She wore this red, silk shirt that was so pretty, and I was wrinkling it with my fists and staining it with my tears, but she didn't care about anything other than holding me."

"What did your dad do?" Dustin asked.

"He was rubbing my back, and when I looked at

him, he was crying, too. It was the only time I ever saw him emotional like that, and it was for me. Later they told me they'd tried for babies for so long, but I was meant to be theirs. Meant to change their life. Except I'm pretty sure it was them who were meant to change my life. If I would've aged out of the orphanage in Russia, I would've had no opportunities. I would've had to work the streets, become a mail order bride, or something else terrifying because who was I? A six-year-old with a hearing impairment and no family, no support system, no future. So my *something real* is I hate when people say bad things about vampires. Sure, some covens are bad, but some crews are bad. Humans have their own villains, too. But nobody says all humans are bad, or all shifters are bad. It's like there is this understanding that only a small part of the population are idiots. With vampires, though, there was never a time where I explained who my parents were and didn't get pitied or fear-filled looks. Never. Not once. All vampires are bad according to everyone. But for me, I got to see the other side. The one where my entire coven, twelve strong, stayed together through all the hard times, fought like a normal family and made-up, spent holidays together, and were strong when one of us struggled. I'm proud to be from the Four Devil's Coven."

"Then why are you trying for the Blackwings? If you're planning on Turning anyway, why leave the family you love? Because let me tell you, if I found that kind of security growing up, I would never leave it."

"It was my parent's suggestion. They said the same to my adopted siblings, Lauren and Enrique. My parents wanted us to experience the sun before we made the decision to Turn."

"They want you to Turn?"

"I thought so, but no, actually. They are the least selfish people I've ever met. Before I came here, my mom sat me down on my bed, held my hands, and told me if my future is in the sunlight, she would be so happy for me. She made me promise to give the Blackwing Crew a chance. She told me if it was up to her, I would stay human or turn shifter so I could have a normal life."

"Normal," Dustin murmured, his sandy-blond brows knitted in confusion.

"Being a shifter is normal to vampires. You get to

sleep at night and do all the fun, normal stuff humans get to do during daylight hours. You don't fear the sun, won't burn to ashes in a stray sunray. You can find normal jobs, make normal friends, and not have to explain yourself every single time someone finds out you're a shifter. She made me promise to give this a chance, so here I am, giving it a chance. And if my hearing wasn't ruined, it would be an easy choice for me."

Dustin looked up from the jeans he was folding with a startled look in his blazing eyes. "What would it be?"

"Now for the make-believe one. You would tell me the mountains of secrets you've kept because you trust me. You would date me, fall hard for me, and someday, you would make love to me and know it was right and claim me. I would claim you back, right before the wolf took me. I would sing at a bar in town at nights, all my own songs, and you would watch from a back corner where you would wear this soft smile because you loved the way my voice sounded. We would be happy here, settled, maybe have a couple of cubs, one who looks like you, and one who looks like me. We would raise them in the crew, give them a good support system, and pray to God they didn't turn out like the other werewolves, but like you instead. Caring. Smart. Empathetic. And every night we would go to sleep in each other's arms, and we would both be happy, even though our starts in life had never pointed us in that direction."

Dustin swallowed hard. He wouldn't meet her eyes. His voiced sounded odd as he said, "Why is that the make-believe part?"

Emma shrugged sadly and folded the final T-shirt. "Instinct. Even us humans have it."

Dustin got really quiet after that. He helped her finish folding laundry and then popped the popcorn in the little microwave above the mini-fridge. He settled under the covers and pulled her close against him, his lips lingering in her hair. He was shaking ever so slightly. She loved the affection. But she hated it because something was wrong, and he wasn't telling her what his body did—that he trusted her.

Lights off, television playing a movie neither one of them cared about, he rubbed her back in gentle circles. On and on Dustin caressed her until her eyelids grew heavy and her body relaxed completely.

And just when she slipped into the space of

dreams, surrounded by Morning Glory meadows and saturated sunlight, a voice whispered to her on the wind. "I'll love you for two thousand years until I see you again."

FIFTEEN

Dustin peeled his shirt off as he made his way to the office. John was sitting with his legs crossed at the ankles on top of the small desk. "Hey Dustin, what can I do you for?"

"John, don't ask questions, but you need to get into one of the motel rooms, lock yourself in, and don't come out no matter what you hear."

John laughed and then frowned, as if he was waiting for the punch line.

Dustin flipped off the light switch, dousing them in darkness. His eyes were probably glowing like a demon's right now. "If you want to live, John, leave. Now."

John dropped the romance novel he'd been

reading and bolted for the key case, chose a set he wanted, then jogged out the front door.

Dustin watched him cross the parking lot and disappear into a room on the end of the L-shape. The asphalt was streaked green and blue, reflecting the neon welcome sign at the entrance of the motel. The ground was wet from the storm that had blown through earlier, and the clouds covering the sky churned with warning. Fucking perfect weather for the hell that was going to go down tonight.

He wasn't a stupid wolf, and he'd hunted with the pack a thousand times. Jace's call earlier demanding that he bring Emma was typical bait-and-switch shit. They were coming for Emma, but their timing had to be right. It had to be immediately after he'd left to meet up with Axton. Knowing Dustin wouldn't risk bringing her himself, Jace would be coming in to retrieve her.

All he had to do was keep Jace human long enough to pummel his dumb face into unconsciousness. And then he was going to kill him.

Only it wasn't Jace's car that showed up a couple minutes later. It was a white SUV with a license plate that read WRCKERS. Shit. Axton, that fucking poop flake, had involved the Wrecker Pack. Or maybe he was taking them over, hell if Dustin knew. He'd never really been a part of making plans. Come to think of it, he'd never really been part of the pack.

Wreckers: three wolves. One medium dominance, the other two brawlers, and Dustin shouldn't be able to take them. *Shouldn't*. But when they exited the vehicle and strode right for Emma's door, something awful happened inside of him. For the first time in his life, Dustin's wolf reared up, snarling, foaming at the mouth, howling, scratching at the inside of his skin, bleeding red fog that tainted his vision. His inner animal was insane as Dustin pushed open the door and loped across the parking lot.

His bare feet were silent against the slick concrete, and he stayed low, upwind of them, using the cars in the parking lot for cover. They didn't speak, only looked at each other with their glowing silver eyes. The alpha twisted his body to the side as if preparing to kick the door in. From the back of his jeans, Dustin pulled the long bowie knife he'd lifted from Logan's room earlier and sprinted for the closest Wrecker. Dustin dragged the blade across his neck deep enough that no amount of wolf healing would fix him in time, and then he was on the alpha next because Jagger was the real threat. Dustin couldn't let him Turn, or he was fucked. He needed him wounded before he went to fur, just to give his wolf a chance in the fight.

Dustin tackled him and slammed the blade at Jagger's face just as he hit the ground. Jagger was fast, though, and gripped his wrist, stopping the blade an inch from his right eye. They would be matched in strength, and he was wasting precious milliseconds with another Wrecker at his back, so Dustin dropped the knife and blasted Jagger in the jaw with his left fist. Two blows were all he got in before he was ripped off and slammed backward into the front of Logan's truck. A headlight broke against his back. It would've hurt if he felt anything right now. The adrenaline was pumping too hard, too fast. *Change! Let me have them!*

Jagger's Second grunted with his Change, and now it was too fucking late anyway. Dustin had to give his body to the wolf and hope for the best. Gritting his teeth, he pushed the Change and caught the Second full in the chest. Fangs and snarling and pain, Dustin fought as though his life depended on it.

No, like Emma's did. He couldn't let them get to her.

When the Second's teeth sank into his shoulder, Dustin clamped down on his neck. It was a bad position, but his wolf was insane with bloodlust right now. Where was Jagger? Dustin gave a glance to Emma's bedroom where Jagger was there boot up like he was about to kick in the door. Fuck! Dustin threw the Second as hard as he could, jerking his muscular neck, and slammed the wolf into Jagger like a dumbfounded bowling pin. Jagger hit the door with his chest.

Dustin didn't give the Second a chance to recover. He was on him before the tan and cream wolf hit the concrete. Teeth and nails and road rash and, God, everything ached, including Dustin's jaws from ripping fur and flesh. There it was. The angle he'd wanted. The death-grip. Something was distracting the Second, and that was fine. Where was Jagger now? Dustin didn't release the Second's neck as the wolf scrabbled for his life. Dustin would endure every bone in his body breaking before he let go this time. Damn though, really...where was Jagger?

Was he already in her room, hurting her? Killing her? Desperation took his wolf, and Dustin ripped the

Second's throat. The wolf gurgled at his feet as Dustin looked up in panic.

Jagger was in wolf form, but he wasn't moving. He lay in a pile at the feet of someone equally terrifying.

Beast stood over Jagger, shoulders heaving, eyes blazing gold, teeth gritted, scars bright red on his face, hungry gaze locked on Dustin. He was too dominant, too broken, couldn't control his animal instinct to attack an injured animal, and Dustin was bleeding bad. He could clearly hear the pit-pat-pit-pat of his own blood on the concrete. It was like a fucking dinner bell for a monster like Beast.

It wasn't Axton who was going to end Dustin.

It was going to be his own damn crew member.

The titan staggered and shook his head hard. "Dustin, Change back."

What? Hell no, he wanted to live. At least as a wolf, he had teeth.

"Now, Dustin, fuck!" Beast grabbed his head. "Can't think, can't think."

And then Winter was there, pushing Beast back off his kill. Off Jagger. "Dustin's ours," she chanted. Winter pointed at Logan behind Beast and yelled,

"Don't you fucking Change!" Logan's eyes were silver and empty. He looked like a serial killer.

With a ragged breath, Dustin forced the Change back and curved in on himself as he coughed blood onto the cement.

"Is it done? Is it done? Right or wrong, Dustin?" Beast asked in an animalistic, feral voice.

"What?"

"I want him," Beast snarled, pushing forward against Winter's hands and lurching for Dustin.

"Get up," Winter commanded Dustin. And then she reared back and slapped Beast so hard the contact echoed through the parking lot.

Dustin staggered to his feet.

"Are you making the right decision?" Beast barked out, his face barely looking human.

Dustin jammed a finger at Emma's door. "I'm making the decision that protects her." She wouldn't hear any of this. He'd made sure to put her hearing aids in the charger before he'd left her room. "I'm making the decision that protects the crew."

Chest heaving, he covered the massive gash across his rib cage to hide it from Beast's view. Warmth trickled through his fingers in a stream.

"I knew it," Logan said. "I fucking called it. She turned him." He pointed at Beast. "You and Kane were wrong."

"What the fuck is going on?" Dustin asked.

"Everyone knows," Winter said, shoving Beast back again. "We know about your meetings. We know you're still Valdoro Pack. Kane wanted to see what you did in the end. He wanted to see if Emma could save you."

Dustin dragged his gaze to her door. What the fuck? So much made sense now. The looks exchanged between Kane and Beast. The feeling like he was a jack-in-the-box and everyone was waiting for him to spring. The Blackwings were waiting on a betrayal. "Does Emma know?"

Winter shook her head and looked sick. "Dark Kane wanted us to let it play out. He ordered us not to tell her."

"It's not over," Dustin gritted out. "This is the Wrecker Pack, not Valdoro." He strode for his car keys, which had been tossed across the sidewalk with his Change. His jeans were in tatters but when he cut to make his way to his room for a new set, Logan tossed him fresh jeans and a T-shirt.

217

"How many?" he asked.

"Two if they haven't dragged in another pack."

"We'll come with you."

"Nope, this is my fight."

"But we're crew—"

"Not yet," he barked out. "Parting with the pack is on me. It always was. I have to do this alone, or I'll never feel okay joining the Blackwings."

"I don't understand," Winter murmured.

"Axton is my alpha." Dustin swallowed bile as he shoved his legs into the jeans. "He's my brother, Winter. He's my responsibility. There's no honor in bringing a crew of titans into pack business. I have to carve my own self out of Valdoro."

Winter made a pitying sound. "Dustin, you're submissive."

"Not tonight." He used the T-shirt to wipe the blood off himself as he jogged to his car. "If..." Fuck, what was he supposed to say to make this okay? "If I don't come back, make Emma understand, okay Winter? Tell her it was for her—all of it."

Winter stepped back like she'd been hit in the stomach, and tears rimmed her glowing eyes. He couldn't do this if Winter made him soft right now, so he slid behind the wheel, jammed the key into the ignition and, skidding on the asphalt, peeled out of the parking lot. He turned up the radio and forced himself not to look back in the rearview mirror at what could've been. At the friends he could've had.

He had to keep his head on straight, and right now, he needed to heal as fast as wolfishly possible and put on one helluva show to get close to Axton. Fuck, he wanted to go back to Emma. To the Blackwings.

Gripping the wheel harder, Dustin slammed his car into the next gear and hit the gas on a straightaway.

A snarl rattled up his throat. He was about to try his damndest to survive tonight because he wanted that make-believe future Emma had talked about more than he'd wanted anything in his life.

Axton was right.

He was the grenade, and the Wreckers had just pulled his fucking pin.

SIXTEEN

Emma woke with a start when something heavy shoved her. For a moment, she didn't know where she was. For a moment, she was still back in the coven house where it should've been daylight hours. But staring at her in the dark were two glowing gold eyes.

She gasped and reached for him, brought her knee up to peg him in the throat, but the sheets kept her trapped.

Two hands held her shoulders pinned to the bed, but then her eyes adjusted slightly to the dark. "Beast?" She could barely hear her own voice.

Shoving the behemoth off her, she reached for her hearing aids in the charger. The light flickered on, nearly blinding her. "Geez," she howled in pain, closing her eyes tightly against the fluorescent light above.

"We have to go." Beast had improved at forming his words carefully for her to read his lips. Why did he look panicked?

Emma scanned the room for Dustin, but he wasn't here. Just Winter, who was on the phone talking too fast for Emma to read her lips, and Logan, leaned against the doorframe with his glowing, nearly-white eyes glued to his mate. Beast pulled her from the bed as she struggled to secure her hearing aids. The air smelled like feeding nights in the coven. The scent of thick iron wafted through the open doorway. What the hell was happening?

She parted her lips to ask, but Beast pulled one of Dustin's T-shirts over her head, shoved a pair of rain boots onto her feet, and dragged her out the door.

"Kane has ordered us off this," Winter said in a frantic voice. "He said Dustin has the right to handle it alone."

"Then fucking stay here," Beast growled out.

Emma nearly tripped over a body. A dead body

that was lying face down, bleeding all over the concrete from his neck. Close by were two dead wolves. "Oh, my gosh," she uttered, nausea curdling in her gut. "Who killed them?"

"Dustin killed those two. Me the other. Emma, we don't have time for this." Beast turned and threw her over his shoulder like a caveman and strode across the parking lot to a blue Ford Raptor.

"Whose truck is this?" she asked as he shoved her into it.

Beast didn't answer until he'd bolted around the other side and climbed in. "It's mine."

"What? Why haven't you been driving then. We've been riding around in Logan's wrecked truck for weeks. Those were bodies back there. Blood. Where are we going?" she asked over the roar of the engine. Her hands were going numb. Maybe she was in shock. "Where is Dustin?"

"Dammit, Beast!" Winter said, banging on the window. He rolled it down as he backed out of the parking spot.

"Are you coming or not?" he gritted out.

"We can't! I heard the order. I can't leave this damn parking lot if I tried. Neither can Logan. Beast, I don't think you should do this. If Dustin's hurt, you won't be able to stop yourself from ending him."

"I'll stop myself."

"You won't!"

"I will! He's supposed to be crew, Winter. I was wrong. Kane's wrong. I'm not officially registered so I give zero fucks about an order from an alpha who isn't my alpha yet. We'll bring him back."

"Alive!" Winter screamed as he peeled out. "Promise me!"

But Beast only gripped the steering wheel and snarled. His phone lit up in the console. He immediately chucked it out the window, but not before Emma caught a glimpse of the name flashing across the caller ID. *Kane.*

"What's going on?" Emma asked.

"Buckle your seatbelt," Beast demanded. His face was terrifying right now.

Emma clicked it quietly into place and clasped her hands in her lap. She wore the oversized T-shirt Beast had dressed her in, but no pants, and it was cold. Gooseflesh covered her entire body.

Beast cast her a quick glance and turned the heat on full-blast. "I forgot you are human," he muttered.

"Beast, where is Dustin?" She was really trying not to have a full-blown panic attack, but Beast was going sixty on a winding and wet road.

"Dustin isn't what you think he is."

"A werewolf?"

"Exactly that, but he isn't crew. He isn't eligible."

"Why not?"

"Because he's still a member of the Valdoro pack. And I don't know exactly how this is going to play out, but my gut tells me you need to be here for whatever goes down." Beast nearly went up on two wheels as he jerked the wheel and skidded across the pavement onto a muddy back road.

"Where are we going?"

"To the place Dustin has been secretly meeting his pack for weeks."

Emma's heart sank down to the pristine floorboard of Beast's truck. "No," she said on a heartbroken breath. "He wouldn't."

"And yet..."

"You followed him?"

"Yep."

"Why?"

"Because like I told you, stalking is fun, and that

wily wolf made the game interesting. His pack is the one who hunted Lexi of the Bloodrunners."

"Air Ryder's mate?"

"That's the one. They hunted her, and the Bloodrunner Dragon burned their asses. Ate most of them, but a few of them got away. Far as I could tell, Dustin didn't join the hunt, and he's being punished by his alpha."

"Axton. His brother."

"Who he still gives fealty to. We would've offed his dumbass earlier, but Rowan demanded we let you try to save him. Kane and I have been prepared to pull the trigger on the weremutt as soon as he picked a side."

"Choose a side? Valdoro Pack or Blackwings?"

"Exactly."

"And has he? Picked a side?"

"Those bodies back there? They were coming after you, Emma." Beast cast her a significant look. "They're dead because he picked you. He chose the Blackwings, too, but he should've asked for backup. He doesn't understand how a crew works." Beast swerved this way and that, avoiding tree stumps and mud holes in the road. "Or fuck, maybe I don't understand. I'm used to a pride, and you breathe, bleed, and die for each other no matter what. Winter and Logan should be in the backseat. The fucking dragons should be in the air headed our way. They're not, so it's you and me. And Dustin if we reach him before those wolves tear him apart."

Beast slammed on the brakes and cut the lights and engine. He reached in the back floorboard and pulled a rifle out of the darkness. "Please, woman, tell me you know how to use one of these. You lived in a coven. Tell me they gave you some form of self-defense training."

Emma realized she knew almost nothing about Beast. This was the most words he'd ever strung together in front of her, and now he had a Raptor, knew everything about Dustin, he'd been Kane's secret right hand in the crew, and had a really nice weapon that he was currently shoving bullets into.

"It's a two-seventy. Yes, I can use it fine, but we're kind of fucked if the rainclouds open up right now. Also it's really low light, so if there isn't an artificial source, this is useless."

Beast handed her the weapon, careful to keep the barrel pointed out the door she'd just kicked open. "Pray for headlights. Let's go. And for God's sake, be quiet. Fucking humans are loud as elephants in the woods."

Emma looked down at the billowing T-shirt and pink galoshes Beast had shoved onto her feet. This right here was a man with impossible expectations. Shaking her head, she slid out of the truck and shouldered the strap of the gun, then closed the door as softly as possible.

She followed Beast quietly, but not two steps into the woods, a long, low howl lifted into the air, then was joined by another, and another, and another, and another...

"Shhhit," Beast muttered. "Valdoro pack should only be two wolves. Axton must've brought in reinforcements. Screw making noise, Human, move those legs."

"What are they doing?" she whispered as she sprinted behind him on a trail he'd obviously used before.

"Hunting. Or killing."

No. No, no, no. Dustin was out here, and she got the awful feeling something bad was happening to him. He'd chosen the side that was going to get him hurt, or worse. Bile crept up her throat as Emma pushed her legs harder. Beast was too fast, his strides twice the length of hers. He was graceful like the big cat that dwelled inside of him and apparently had fantastic night vision.

Up ahead, she could make out light through the trees. Her legs and lungs burned, but still she pushed herself faster, squishing through the mud, slipping and sliding and scrabbling for purchase as Beast lengthened the distance between them. Beast disappeared into the night, and Emma had a horrifying moment of panic. Up until the point he grabbed her ankle and dragged her down beside him. He'd flattened down behind some brush, so she settled the rifle on a strip of grass in front of them and did the same. Through the branches, she could see them.

In the high beams of several cars, there was a loose circle of wolves, ducking in and out, dodging, some lowering to their bellies before standing again, ears erect, lips curled back. Their teeth weren't white, though. They were red. The howling and yipping was constant.

The circle thinned in front of Emma and Beast,

and she gasped at what she saw. A massive black wolf was tangled in a vicious fight with two gray wolves.

Emma bolted upward, but Beast dragged her down and slammed a hand over her mouth, then shook his head and gave her the deadliest look she'd ever seen.

Read my lips, he mouthed. *There is no honor among wolves. He's giving them hell, but they will eventually kill him. Which one is Axton?*

She shook her head. *Dustin never told me what he looked like.*

Fuck. I'm going in. If you figure out which one the alpha is... Beast gripped the barrel of her rifle and shook it gently, then raised his eyebrows. *End it.*

Okay. Beast! She grabbed his arm. *They'll kill you.*

Beast shrugged and smiled sadly. *All I have to live for is the D-Team*. He hesitated a moment more, stood and pulled off his shirt, and then strode into the clearing.

His battle cry tapered into a roar, and the massive, broken lion he kept tucked inside of him ripped out of his skin. Some of the wolves scattered for a second, but as Beast charged, the pack rallied.

Emma couldn't take her eyes from Dustin. He

was brutal, and already three lay dead around him. He was holding his own with two, and with Beast taking heat off him, he was moving more freely, snapping and snarling and connecting with flesh so fast he blurred from one position to the next. A submissive animal shouldn't be able to do what he was doing, but perhaps the pack had finally broken him. Perhaps they'd finally pushed him too far.

She had to figure out which one was Axton. He couldn't be one of the dead ones, or the wolves would've pulled off the attack. Unless the alpha of the other pack here was calling all the shots now. God, she wished she understood pack dynamics better, but Dustin had always seemed to want to live in the here-and-now and forget about pack stuff when he was with her. Now she realized he had been protecting them in a way. She hated their hold on him.

Dustin and Beast were fighting side by side, mauling the wolves as they lunged. More were trotting in from the woods to the east, though. Axton had called in multiple packs, and all for what? To kidnap her? To kill her? No. The psychopath had pulled in packs to kill his own flesh and blood brother. She fucking hated them.

Emma pulled the hammer back and shoved a bullet into the chamber, took off the safety, and carefully aimed the rifle through the branches. She couldn't hit a single one or the ricochet could be catastrophic. The scope was picking up some light, but she was limited on where she could aim. Several parked cars had their headlights on, but even if she could get a clear shot, Dustin and Beast were everywhere. Two killing machines with empty eyes and blood-soaked muzzles. Dustin's fur was matted, but if he was hurt, he wasn't acting like it. He fought without a limp, fought without any impairment—just lethal precision.

He'd joked about being submissive, even told her about hating that part of himself, but he wasn't giving his neck to anyone tonight.

Dustin was war in motion.

The brush rustled behind her, and with a gasp, Emma rolled over onto her back, dragging the gun with her. The wolf that ran from the ferns was hideous. He was a mottled black and gray wolf with white eyes and burn scars down one side of his body. He looked like he had mange since his hair only grew in patches. His lips were curled back, exposing razor sharp teeth. He was lanky, but bigger than Dustin's wolf by several inches. His face was the stuff of nightmares. Axton, she would venture to guess.

No time to look in the scope, she lifted the barrel and pulled the trigger. The butt of the rifle slammed against her shoulder because she hadn't the time to position it right, but that was nothing compared to the pain of the weight of the snarling wolf. Axton slipped on his back leg where her shot had landed, and that injury was buying her time. Emma fought like some wild thing, using the gun to keep his jaws off her neck. "Dustin!" she screamed.

Desperate to live, Emma's system filled with adrenaline as she kicked against Axton, and pushed against the gun. Just as her strength failed and Axton lunged forward, something dark sailed over the brush behind her and barreled into her attacker. Axton flew sideways and spun into a tree, but Dustin wasn't done with him. He attacked viciously. Beast roared behind her, and the air filled with the howling and barking of wolves. Emma should've been cheering Dustin on, happy for him that he was ending this, that he wasn't on his belly begging to be a part of a pack that didn't deserve him. She should've been fully immersed in the moment, but all she could do was stare at the seeping bite mark on her hand.

Tears streamed out of her eyes to her cheeks and slipped down, down until they made pattering sounds on the dry leaves beneath her knees. Axton was lying on the ground now, eyes full of hate on his brother who stood over him, crimson teeth bared and poised to finish him. Dustin hesitated, though, and she got it. Even if he was traitorous and evil, Axton was his brother.

Burning pain drifted up her veins from the bite mark, and she clutched it to her stomach as if that would stop the excruciating sensation. "Dustin," she whimpered.

His glowing green and blue eyes crashed onto her.

"I'm sorry," she said mindlessly. It hurt so bad. "I'm sorry." She held out her hand. *Pit-pat, pit-pat.*

She couldn't even open her hand anymore. It was frozen with pain, as if she was in a fire she couldn't escape. As if she was a vampire in the sun, but that would never be now. Not when the wolf was devouring her body.

Dustin looked back at his brother, and a

horrifying snarl left his lips. Axton huffed a sound that resembled a wolfish laugh. Laughing? He thought this was funny? Wreaking havoc on Kane's Mountains, using his brother, planning and plotting Dustin's death, and now this? Stealing her chance at turning vamp, stealing her chance at hearing like everyone else. Stealing her chance to sing.

Dustin leapt onto him, and Emma ripped her gaze away when he jerked Axton's neck. There was a sharp whine, and then nothing. The pain was dizzying, and all around her was the barking and howling of the wolves, as though they were calling the monster from her soul.

A panther screamed in the woods, a bear roared, and across the sky streaked two monstrous dragons. Perhaps she was dreaming. Perhaps she was still back in the motel and would wake up from this nightmare whole again.

Head spinning, she fell backward, but where she expected to hit the ground hard, Dustin's arms were there, cradling her back and head.

He was in his human form, but he looked like hell. Beautiful hell. Cut and bitten, covered in seeping crimson, his long hair matted and plastered to his blood-spattered face, his eyes glowing, Dustin looked like a warrior. No, he was a warrior.

"Beast," she murmured, her arms seizing with the fire in her veins.

"Fighting." Dustin looked up toward the sounds of yipping and whining and chaos. "All of the Blackwings are fighting but the dragons. They're waiting."

"For what?"

Dustin leveled her with a look. "For vengeance. They'll be eating ashes tonight."

"It hurts," she whispered.

Dustin's eyes rimmed with deep emotion, and he looked away. "I know, Em." He swallowed hard and looked sick. "This is all my fault."

"I don't want his wolf, Dustin. Not his."

He dragged his misty-eyed gaze back to her. "I can call your coven. My phone is in the car. Maybe they can get here in time."

She shook her head. Sweet wolf for trying to give her what she wanted. "That option has passed. I can feel it in me." She arched her back as she felt her bones breaking. Emma sobbed, "Dustin, I want a wolf from you. Please."

A tear streaked through the blood on his cheek. He pulled her against his chest. And right before he sank his teeth into her shoulder, he whispered, "I'm so sorry." And then there was deep, aching pain.

The fire blasted down her nerve endings, but she didn't fight this one. This wolf she wanted. Dustin was sorry, and so was she for how things had turned out, but right now it felt imperative that she was Turned by Dustin, not Axton. Some deep-rooted instinct told her she could be okay if Dustin Turned her. She didn't want to be a monster. Her entire torso was engulfed in pain now, but this was how it should've been. Dustin was rushing to take her shoes off, her shirt...her hearing aids. She would still need those. Emma sobbed harder as she curled in on the pain expanding like a sickening fog down through her stomach.

There was fire around them. Dual flames blasted into the clearing behind her. She could smell the smoke and more. She could smell the dragon's gas and hear the click of their firestarters. Agony rippled through her, warring with the pain in her arms until a new and brighter pain took over.

"Let her have you," Dustin murmured, rocking

Emma's body and stroking her hair away from her face.

Winter was there, a black panther, pacing a few feet behind Dustin, her glowing eyes gold and trained on Emma.

Let her have you.

Massive and hollow-eyed, face and claws covered in blood, Logan's bear lumbered in behind Winter.

Let her have you.

And then Beast was there, human, bitten up, bleeding, eyes glowing gold still. He felt terrifying. Was this what Dustin was always talking about? Could she feel dominance now?

Let her have you.

Emma closed her eyes and reached for the wolf. The good one that was light and born willingly. The one Dustin had given her, not the dark creature that sat snarling within her and ready for violence. Not the monstrous creature Axton had tried to turn her into.

With a gasp, Emma held onto the good pieces of herself and ripped apart.

SEVENTEEN

Emma was the most beautiful creature Dustin had ever seen. She stood there in the headlights, legs splayed like a newborn colt, eyes a fierce green and locked on him. Her coat was thick and striking with cream points and a light gray saddle. Her ears were erect, and her lips were drawn back over her teeth. She approached slowly, head down, steps unsteady as her massive paws flattened against the mud. She gave narrow-eyed looks to the D-Team, then trained those blazing green eyes back on Dustin.

Shit, she was about to maul him, and he was too devoted to her to lift a single fang to hurt her. She could gut him right now, and he would let it happen.

Axton's wolf had won. That much was clear from

the snarl in her throat and the heaviness that wafted from her. Emma climbed over his legs, opened her jaws, and bit into his shoulder, shredded it. Dustin grunted and waited for her to move to his neck and end it all.

But she didn't.

Emma released him and did something that made no sense at all. She licked his wound over and over, cleaning it. Panting at the pain, he looked to Logan, but the bear huffed a deep breath and herded Winter into the woods. Beast stood suddenly and strode away into the shadows, and the dragons dipped this way and that into the woods, devouring ashes, devouring the packs that had joined forces to destroy Dustin.

Emma buried her massive face against his chest and whined, her tail wagging slowly, and it hit him. Axton's wolf hadn't won. Emma had.

Her first act as a werewolf wasn't violence. It wasn't vengeance for what had been done to her.

Instead, Emma—his beautiful, loyal, fearless Emma—had claimed him back.

EIGHTEEN

This body didn't make sense yet, but it would. Her stance was too wide as she tried to keep her balance, especially with Dustin's grip in the scruff of her neck. His face was buried in her fur, and over and over again, he heaved breath. He'd been through hell tonight. They both had.

She'd already fallen in love with him, but here, in this body where all her senses were heightened and on alert, she became hopelessly devoted to him. He smelled so familiar. Fur and Dustin. Blood, too, but that was an afterthought. Perhaps it was the bite she'd given him that was causing the warm sensation in her chest right now, or perhaps it was that he smelled so sad and so happy all at once. Guilt for what had happened to her, but more potent than that, love. He'd chosen her without hesitation. She'd asked for his wolf, and there had been the barest flicker of a relieved smile there on his lips. He was her world now. Her pack, her crew, her mate.

Mine, she tried to say, but it came out a high-pitched whine that hurt her ears.

Everything was so loud in this body, so crisp. Every leaf rustling in the storm wind, every soft pattering rain drop, every hitched breath from Dustin.

"I heard the gunshot, and I thought I was going to lose you," he rumbled in a gravelly voice. "I thought I wasn't going to get to Axton in time. Why did you come for me, you crazy woman? I told you to be careful, not run into danger."

She whined again and licked his face. *I would do anything for you, just like you would do anything for me.*

A precise line of fire blasted the earth behind Dustin and ate up Axton's body. The wind grew to hurricane strength, and Dustin shielded her protectively. In a moment, it was done. All that was left was Kane's terrifying dragon arching upward with battered demon wings that stretched as wide as a mountain. Where Axton had lain, there was nothing but a deep divot of charred earth.

Dustin was free, but his eyes held a thousand ghosts as he looked at the burned earth. Emma's heart ached for him. He'd had to kill his own brother, and no matter that Axton deserved death, it would be a mark on Dustin's soul forever. Emma wished she could take that pain into herself so he wouldn't suffer.

Winter's panther screamed again from the woods. She was calling Emma, calling the crew. Above, the dragons were monstrous, lifting on the air currents until they disappeared into the thick, roiling storm. Lightning flashed and illuminated their dark silhouettes in the clouds. To Human Emma, it would've been a terrifying sight, but to Wolf Emma, it was beautiful. Those were her dragons. Beast had thought the crew failed them, but they had come. *Breathe, bleed, and die for each other, no matter what.* Perhaps this crew was more like a pride than the battle-hardened Beast had realized.

"Emma," Dustin murmured in the softest voice.

She ripped her gaze away from the sky and

searched his eyes. *What Dustin?*

A slow smile transformed his face as he cocked his head. "You can hear me," he said in the barest whisper.

Emma perked her ears, flattened them, and perked them again. Winter, Logan, and Beast were moving through the woods, just beyond the shadows. She couldn't see them in the dark, but she could hear exactly where they were and smell that it was them. She could hear Dustin's breath and his racing heartbeat. She could hear her own.

She'd known her hearing would be improved in this body, but she hadn't realized it would be perfect. She wanted to cry and scream and laugh, and then cry some more. She spun a quick circle and blasted down onto her front paws, butt up in the air, tail wagging for her mate. *You did good Dustin. Really good.*

"Listen," he murmured. Dustin cupped her face gently and raised his eyebrows. "Listen. We always knew the animal would be able to hear. Your human hearing will be improved, but it might not be like this. We won't know until you Change back."

Emma pranced from foot to foot. *How do I*

Change back?

"Wait." When Dustin chuckled, his smile was stunning.

Home is where you rest your bones. No. Home was in Dustin's smile. The real ones he made for her.

Dustin stood, his muscles flexing with the movement. His eyes were so pretty right now in the dark, glowing blue and seafoam green. "Before you Change back, and before we find out either way how your hearing will be in your human body, I want to show you something. Okay?"

She yipped excitedly a few times. There was too much pent-up energy in her body. She could hear Winter purring now. Emma wanted to tackle her with wolf hugs and bite her. Not to make her bleed, just to tell her she loved her. A love bite. She would bite Logan and Beast, too, and if they tried to kill her, she would just run away. She would be fast in this body. *Show me!*

She bolted unsteadily to the tree line, then back for Dustin. She was starting to get the hang of this body. *Come on! I want to see and hear everything!*

Dustin grunted and Changed into his beautiful black wolf with the eyes she adored. She didn't like the pained sound in her mate's throat, though, so she licked his face, because instinct said face licks would make anything better. She could lick him all night. She was going to do that. Lick him until he was happy, but wait! Dustin let off a warning growl and clamped his teeth onto her neck. Whoo, he was serious. And sexy. She liked his teeth. He gave good love bites. Emma barked excitedly about a dozen times in a row until Dustin let off a strange, long yip and trotted off toward the D-Team. He stopped at the tree line and waited, eyes locked on hers, face somber.

He was stunning in this form. There was no color variation in his fur, and he wasn't mottled like Axton had been. She could see him so much better in this body. He was pure black with a thick barrel chest and long, powerful legs, giant paws, and a thick tail that swished languidly as she approached. He probably had fifty pounds on her wolf. *Mine, mine, mine. Dark Wolf, bright soul. My Dustin.* Emma was a greedy wolf. She would bite anyone who looked at him. *Hi Dustin!* She rubbed up his body like a prancing cat, and he huffed a wolfish laugh, then trotted off into the woods, careful to step around the scorch marks.

Careful to avoid the last remaining evidence his psychotic brother had existed on this earth. Emma sniffed it. Bad. Smelled like evil. Dustin wasn't like him. She'd gotten the good one, not the cull pup. She'd gotten the one who grew up to be a dependable, protective man.

The rain sounded beautiful. Her ears twitched in every direction with the rain pattering against fern leaves. Dustin had warned her not to get her hopes up in her human body. It wouldn't be like this. She still had missing parts in that body. She would still have impairment, but at least the tradeoff was this. At least her wolf could hear. She wanted to cry again. Why were her emotions so up and down right now?

Winter hissed as she trotted by.

I love you, too. Emma veered off and chased her for a love bite, but Winter bolted up a tree. Tricky kitty. Emma pranced back and forth on her front two paws and barked, but Winter sat on a branch out of reach, her long, black tail curved down gracefully, her eyes glowing gold in the dim light.

Dustin circled around her, herding her. He wasn't as tricky as Winter. She could see exactly what he was doing. He wanted to show her something, so she gave in. *Bye Winter!* Oh! The sleek cat jumped in front of Emma and startled her.

Winter was big, and her claws were out as she slunk into step beside her. *Hi.* She ran her whiskered cheek against Emma's muzzle once.

Emma tried to lick her, but Winter ducked out of the way and swatted her with a massive paw. Didn't hurt. Logan was here now, an enormous dark-furred grizzly, striding in the woods parallel to them. He smelled like blood and brokenness. Emma loved him, too.

Beast was human, but Emma wanted to sniff him, so she bounded up to him and barked a bunch so he would memorize what she sounded like. *You're welcome.*

Beast narrowed his eyes down at her. His face looked painful, all scarred up on one side and perfect on the other. He lunged like he would attack her, but he didn't smell mad, not really, so Emma held her ground and wagged her tail. He was all cut up, and the rain that splattered on his skin made red rivers down his torso. *You're my friend. You helped me save the one I love.*

Beast snarled, but there was no venom behind it.

With an annoyed glance at the group behind them, he sighed and brushed his fingertips over the fur on her head once. "Now shove off," he muttered.

But she didn't miss it. He'd smiled. Only for a moment, but it was there, and it counted. Tonight was the best. Except...she really wasn't going to be a vampire now, and maybe she would never sing... A wave of memories hit her at once. The longing to be in choir with her school friends, playing guitar to her lyrics and barely being able to hear the music. Her voice, always off-key and out of her control. Always slurred, no matter how hard she worked on it. All of the times she cried on her bed and wished she could sing like the people she wrote songs for.

Her emotions were so overwhelming in this body. A soft whine left her as she really thought about the blow she'd been dealt. She'd gotten the wolf, but it had come with a price. What if her hearing was just the same when she Changed back to a human?

And then Dustin was there, right beside her, big and strong and steady. He drew in front of her and blocked her path. Was this what he wanted to show her? Emma looked around, but there was nothing special about this clearing. It was circular and surrounded by towering trees that had vines dangling from their branches. Despite the October chill, everything was still lush and green, and the moon had peeked out from the clouds just enough to douse the forest in hues of blue. It was beautiful—breathtaking really—but it was just like the other woods they'd been walking through.

And then everything changed in an instant.

Beside her, Dustin arched his neck back slowly, a howl lifting from him as he closed his eyes. Emma stood there utterly shocked at the sound. So pure. So perfect. Her fur stood up all over her body. When Dustin's note tapered, he lowered his muzzle to hers and opened his eyes. He said so much with that look.

I love you. This is the gift that comes with the wolf. Are you ready to sing?

Buried in emotion, Emma lowered her head.

Dustin lifted a howl again, but this one was different. It was lower, louder. It called to her in ways she didn't understand. It drew her wolf up and made her want to...sing.

Emma blinked rapidly as she looked at the D-Team. The dragons moved in the woods, their backs high above the trees. It wasn't just the D-Team here anymore. This was the Blackwing Crew, here to listen to her first song.

Dustin was holding his note, head back, calling her.

With a deep inhale, Emma made an unsteady yipping sound and let it taper into a deep howl her wolf just knew how to make. She held the note. Perfect tone. Emotion clogged her throat, so she cut it off. Dustin took a breath and sang again. Feeling like this moment was everything, Emma threw her head back and joined him, lifting a note of her own slowly to match his. All was quiet except for their duet. The others watched and waited and listened, and Emma was lost on the drifting notes she and Dustin sang together. It was the most beautiful song she'd ever heard, and she was a part of it.

With the wave of raw emotion that washed over her, something happened to her body. It buckled and Changed. It hurt, but it was fast. And within moments, she was on her knees in the grass, human, naked, sobbing. And then Dustin was there, holding her, cupping her head gently, rocking them back and forth. He was murmuring something, but her hearing wasn't as good in this body. She could hear better than she used to, but it was comparable to having her hearing aids in.

This had been her nightmare growing up. All this time, this had been her biggest fear, that she would have to accept the impairment. But maybe it was time to do just that. It was time to stop looking toward some perfect future where she would be able to hear like everyone else. It was time to accept herself just as she was. At least she had the wolf. Emma rested her cheek against Dustin's chest and cried, hugging him tightly. Her loss warred with her joy.

Hands touched her back, rested there, and the murmurs of her friends filled her heart with belonging. She looked up, and they were there, the crew. All of them.

Winter was crying. "You sounded beautiful."

So Emma wasn't perfect. Maybe that hadn't been her destiny. Maybe this one broken thing made her fit in better with her monsters—Dark Kane, Rowan, Beast, Winter, Logan...Dustin. None of them were perfect either, but they were still worthy of love.

Her dreams weren't crushed. They were just different now.

So she wouldn't be some great singer in the bar or on the radio.

Instead, she would be the singer of the woods with the wolf she loved.

NINETEEN

Emma stepped deeper into the landscaping and upended the watering can over the fall mums Dustin had planted for her on the one-month anniversary of her Turning.

So much had changed in four tiny weeks. No longer was the motel home, but she and Dustin had officially registered to the Blackwing Crew and were now living in a doublewide they'd bought together in the Blackwing Mobile Park. It was so different from the coven house where chaos reigned. This life was quiet, full of those moments that made her draw up and pay attention to the here and now instead of the what-could-bes of the future.

Winter and Logan lived in the trailer next door

and were chattering happily on their front porch swing. Logan laughed a lot now. At the very end of the trailer park, Beast had set up his singlewide trailer with a big front porch where he spent a lot of nights staring at the stars and drinking. Alone. Always alone if he had his way.

He'd set the penis-shaped napkin trophy in his front window and built a fence around his trailer with a *No Trespassing* sign posted on it. He was sitting on his porch now, the king of his lonely domain. At least when she lifted her hand and waved to him, Beast nodded back from where he sat in a bag chair and lifted a beer in a silent cheers before he gave his attention to the sunset again.

Rowan was kind as ever, and little by little, Dark Kane was opening up to the crew, to Dustin especially. He'd even pulled her mate in for a mannish hug at the bar last night, and they'd spent half the night sitting next to each other shooting the shit. She'd thought there would always be tension there since Dustin had been placed in these mountains to betray him, but Kane had forgiven him as far as she could tell. Rowan probably had helped with that. She'd thanked Emma for saving Dustin, whatever that meant. Dustin was the one who had saved her in so many ways.

It was November now, and frigid, so as the breeze kicked up, Emma wrapped her sweater tighter around her shoulders.

"Cold?" Dustin asked from the porch stairs where he sat. He liked watching her in the garden. She wasn't as skilled as his mom, and likely wouldn't ever be, but the mums did feel a bit like her little babies. She'd started talking to them when no one was looking.

"Cold? Not really, but it's habit. I'm still used to being chilly all the time." Emma stood back and admired the burnt-orange and yellow flowers. While she was at it, she studied the doublewide trailer that she and Dustin had been sleeping in for a week now. "I still can't believe we're here."

"What do you mean?" There was a smile in Dustin's voice, and he came to stand behind her, wrapped his arms around her chest, and kissed her neck.

"I mean in this moment. Thinking about all we've been through and all that happened takes my breath away. This feels like a fairy tale, but we're the ones who got the happy ending, you know?"

He chuckled and plucked her skin gently with his lips. "Trust me, Shortcake, you have me counting my blessings a dozen times a day."

"I have to tell you something."

Dustin went rigid behind her. "Okay," he murmured.

She spun slowly in his arms to face him. The sunset behind him made his eyes look even more striking. She stroked a wayward strand of his soft hair from his face. "You once told me werewolves say home is where you rest your bones. Do you still feel like that?"

Dustin huffed a relieved sigh and kissed the inside of her palm. Tucking his chin to his chest, he shook his head, then jerked his chin at the trailer behind her. "Home is where I bone you."

"Stop, I'm trying to be serious."

"Me too, woman. Home is wherever you are. You and the Blackwings. This house. These mountains. Lately, I've been getting all fucking choked up just watching the smile on your face when you're in the garden. When you look and smell happy, that's home. You're happy here, so..." He looked around the park and huffed a laugh. "A trailer park full of psychopaths is home, and I wouldn't have it any other way."

Emma stood on her tiptoes and pressed her lips to his. The kiss was a soft, slow one, where he loosened up over time and dragged his hand up her back and into her hair.

Dustin angled his face and brushed his tongue against hers, then eased back to rest his forehead on hers. "Tell me you're happy."

"You know I am."

"But I like it when you say it. When you tell me I make you happy."

Tears burned her eyes, and she nuzzled her face against his cheek. Softly, she murmured, "You make me happier than anything. Do you know what my prized possession is?"

"My dick?"

Emma giggled. "Close. It's a packet of Morning Glory seeds, sitting in the bowl on the table near the door, just waiting to be planted in the spring. I'll get to see them bloom every day, Dustin. You gave me sunlight without knowing it. You gave me a happier life than I could've imagined. You changed the course of everything. I just wanted to say thank you. Thank you for being you, for being strong, for protecting me, and for going against your pack to keep me safe." Her voice broke, so she swallowed hard so she could say this next part, the important part, clearly. "And thank you for the wolf."

"You aren't angry?"

"I know that's what you expect of me. I know that's what you're thinking when you watch me late at night. You're waiting for me to break down, but no. I love my wolf. I get to hear everything when I'm running the woods with you. You gave me the ability to sing, just in a different way than I'd expected. Maybe it's not how I planned things, but this is exactly where I'm supposed to be. In your arms, in this moment. You're my best friend, Dustin. You gave me everything and asked for nothing in return."

"Well, I asked you for blow jobs in return."

Emma snorted and conceded, "You asked me for nothing but blow jobs in return."

Kane's Bronco bounced and bumped under the mobile park sign. Rowan waved out the passenger side window like she hadn't seen them in days. Laughing, Emma dashed her hand under her eyes and waved back.

Today was Saturday, or as Kane had deemed it, D-Team Sucks Saturday.

Dustin, Logan, Beast, and Kane had built a sprawling barbecue pit and covered gazebo on the empty side of the trailer park. Every Saturday they cooked out as a crew because Dark Kane was beginning to realize the importance of them bonding.

Beast tossed his empty can onto his chair and jogged down his porch stairs. Logan gave Winter a piggy-back ride toward where Kane was parking near the covered area. Dustin pulled the watering can from Emma's hand and jerked his chin. "You ready to go hang out with the monsters?"

She slipped her hand into his and corrected him. "Our monsters."

Oh, it would be like every other Saturday. They would cook out, laugh, but then someone would fuck it all up in true D-Team fashion, and everyone would fight and bleed each other. Rowan or Winter or Emma would laugh first. They would all settle down, Change together, and then roam the woods with the dragons flying above.

The Blackwings were a beautiful disaster.

Dustin looked over his shoulder at her and smiled—the real one she coveted so much.

And with one hand, in simple alphabet, he signed something that made all their struggles to get to this moment worth it.

You make me happy, too.

BLACKWING WOLF

Want more of these characters?

Blackwing Wolf is the second book in a three book series based in Kane's Mountains.

Check out these other books from T. S. Joyce.

Blackwing Defender
(Kane's Mountains, Book 1)

Blackwing Beast
(Kane's Mountains, Book 3)

Also, if you would like to read Kane and Rowan's story, it can be found in the final book of the Harper's Mountains series.

Blackwing Dragon
(Harper's Mountains, Book 5)

About the Author

T.S. Joyce is devoted to bringing hot shifter romances to readers. Hungry alpha males are her calling card, and the wilder the men, the more she'll make them pour their hearts out. She werebear swears there'll be no swooning heroines in her books. It takes tough-as-nails women to handle her shifters.

Experienced at handling an alpha male of her own, she lives in a tiny town, outside of a tiny city, and devotes her life to writing big stories. Foodie, wolf whisperer, ninja, thief of tiny bottles of awesome smelling hotel shampoo, nap connoisseur, movie fanatic, and zombie slayer, and most of this bio is true.

Bear Shifters? Check

Smoldering Alpha Hotness? Double Check

Sexy Scenes? Fasten up your girdles, ladies and gents, it's gonna to be a wild ride.

For more information on T. S. Joyce's work,
visit her website at
www.tsjoyce.com

Made in the USA
San Bernardino, CA
18 December 2016